MAIN STREET

Anyone's Town, Everyone's Forever

Stephen W. Hoag, Ph.D.

authorHOUSE

AuthorHouse™
1663 Liberty Drive
Bloomington, IN 47403
www.authorhouse.com
Phone: 833-262-8899

Published by AuthorHouse 08/31/2022

ISBN: 978-1-6655-6888-3 (sc)
ISBN: 978-1-6655-6889-0 (hc)
ISBN: 978-1-6655-6887-6 (e)

Library of Congress Control Number: 2022915518

Contents

Prologue

This powerful romance novel, once read, will remain in your soul forever as the characters set within this tale of the age of innocence will steal a piece of your heart.

Each of us is a novel unto ourselves with endless chapters of triumph and tragedy. With each incidental instance that we are touched by someone in life, sometimes with nothing more than a walkthrough, our individual saga is changed, and the expanse of our frame of reference is altered.

The story about to unfold comes to life on a street in "any town" in America, a "tableau vivant" (a living picture), where a group of young people begins to define themselves in that period known as the high school years. There are many clinical definitions and technical labels for this wisp of one's lifetime, but in the reminiscences within most of us, the high school years fill our memory luggage. The community of Wallingford, Connecticut, is used as the scaffolding of this tale as the author writes deeply and explicitly about a street within the community he adores.

The characters in this narrative are amalgamations of many real people with names that might remind or mislead the reader of someone they remember all too well. Although this romantically woven fable is fictitious, each twist and turn could and probably did occur in your town—on your Main Street—and in your life.

For this fable of romance and revelation, we peer into the hearts and minds of a few dozen high school students, each seeking moments to fill their growing vessels of youthful passion and desire while discovering their personal levels of giving and kindness.

With all the fleeting lessons in language arts, math, science, and history, drilled and demonstrated during the secondary school years, what endures as this story will elucidate are the forever feelings and relationships that grow strong, never to be shaken. In this tale, young hearts will spring forth like a babbling stream and rekindle your memories of times long since evaporated but impossible to exfoliate on the landscape of your heart.

As your eyes will read, this high school is a key player in this story, in many ways, one of the living characters that entwine, fuses, and provides context for the many personalities who come to life when individual dreams, schemes, and drama are allowed to breathe anywhere at any time.

Rather deliberately, no date or decade defines the time domain of this novel as these incredible characters might be from any era, but in immersing oneself in the story, you might be most comfortable setting down in the 1950s or 1960s.

The heart-stopping conclusion of this novel will spark a degree of envy as your heart stretches to ask, "Why not me?" Revel in this story as it has happened to those in your life or *you*.

Chapter 1

Main Street

Anyone's Town, Everyone's Forever

The dawn of a crisp spring day beckons as a light rain dots the tan-colored cement slabs of the sidewalks bordering Main Street. Ah yes, Main Street—every town has one. It sometimes brandishes the town's name followed by the generic term street, avenue, or boulevard; but it always represents a long connected road with historic homes, probably the town hall, the library, small retail shops, and the requisite banks and insurance offices.

"Main Street," the location in every town where directions to everyplace else begin. Walk north along Main, passing the high school on your left. When you cross Main and Center intersection, cross Center and keep walking straight. You'll see the old town well on the corner. You'll see Caplan's and St. Paul's Church on the opposite side of the street. About one hundred yards beyond that is the State Armory. You can't miss it.

Beyond a geographic reference point, Main Street is a slice of history for the town. From South to North Main, both sides of the street are lined with the domiciles of long-ago prominent people: bankers, writers, doctors, lawyers, elected leaders, farmers, industrialists, journalists, and indeed, faces framed by the windows and doors of their homes.

It is impossible to walk or drive along Main Street and not gape at the remarkable variety of historical architectural designs as each structure is dissimilar from any other. The very nature of these unique homes makes Main Street a perpetual celebration of the town.

Against the trappings of Main Street, a very different story of celebration is about to unfold. This is a tale of youthful hearts, minds, and eyes as they blend together in those years between childhood and adulthood. For many a young person, the high school seasons, those mid-teenage years of life, will be reflected upon as the best years of one's life. It is a period of discovery, self-examination, and desire for everyone.

Here on Main Street, magic will take place, love will blossom, a heart or two may be broken yet repaired, and unforgettable moments created through the unbridled creativity of youth will emerge.

Chapter 2

Meet Lefky

The 7:40 a.m. warning bell for the start of the high school day was of such blaring decibel level that breakfast table settings on the kitchen tables of the residents of Main Street would rattle. If you happened to be a student walking to school from as far away as Ward Street to the south or Christian Street to the north, you knew you had better put a hustle in your steps as the homeroom period would begin in ten minutes, and no one wanted to be late. That would mean detention and having to face the Vice Principal, *nasty ole* Mr. Pappas, breathing down your neck in detention hall after school.

The warning bell prompted students to begin lining up at their respective gender-specific entrances. Gabbing students at the girls and boys entrances were winding around to the wide front walkway leading to the pillared front doors of the school. Entrances that students were not allowed to enter through but could exit at the conclusion of the school day. They were awaiting the 7:50 a.m. bell, which signaled the girls and boys doors opened by a teacher on duty.

Students who drove to school added to the morning noise on Main Street as many would rev their engines, passing in front of the school as they looked for parking spaces along Main or behind the school in the parking lot that, at maximum, could hold sixty vehicles.

On this particular morning, Susan Adams, a junior, scurried along the eastern side of Main, blocks away from the school; as a two-tone blue car pulled up close to the curb,

3

and winding down the driver's side window, a voice called out, "Suz, want a lift?"

Susan was immediately taken aback as no one ever calls her "Suz," a nickname she hated, and most other students and family knew she detested that handle.

Maintaining her quick stride, she looked into the car and recognized the driver as Arthur Lefkowitz, otherwise known as Lefky. Returning the nickname (insult), she called back, "Hey, *Lefty*, I'd rather hitch a ride with a car full of circus clowns."

Now the slick-ass Arthur is incensed, returning fire, "*No one* ever calls me 'Lefty.' My name is *Lefky*."

Lefkowitz, never one to avoid verbal cross-swords, answers, "Sue-*san*, c'mon, I'll get you there on time. You can sit in the back seat, and I will be like a chauffeur."

Fearing the thought of being late and having detention, Susan bears up under the nickname attack and reluctantly gets in the car in the front bench seat. Once inside, she hugs the passenger side door to avoid getting any closer to Lefky than absolutely necessary, keeping her gaze straight ahead.

With only a few blocks from the high school, Lefky pulls out onto Main, but his eyes saunter to the right to Susan, wearing a short black and white sweater dress with a cropped cashmere cardigan sweater. She is very aware of his attention to her and is ready to jump out of the car as soon as she pulls over to park. In a gesture of kindness, inconsistent for the fast-talking, "always on the make" Lefkowitz pulls over across the school as Susan opens the door, crossing Main and yelling back over her shoulder a disingenuous, "Thanks!"

Susan makes it to homeroom on time, but as for Lefky, a more uneven outcome awaits. A junior, Arthur Lefkowitz, has come to understand the system and process of the high school, and he plays it with the skill of a master craftsman. Proceeding to drive around the back of the school, Lefky finds a narrow parking space near the school dumpster. Exiting his car, failing to lock the vehicle or wind up the window, he heads to a back double-door entrance where the janitors take out the trash and deliveries are made.

As luck would have it, one of the janitors, Mr. Costello, is taking out trash boxes from the cafeteria, and Lefky immediately offers to help him, knowing well that this would make him more than just a little late for homeroom period.

Lefky carried two boxes of empty number ten tin cans to the dumpster, and then quickly made his way to the back door to climb up the two flights of stairs, down the hallway to his homeroom, 223. Entering the room, his homeroom teacher, Ms. Pellington, a first-year teacher who looked the age and appearance of most any other female student in the school, bellowed, "Lefkowitz, you are late. You have a detention."

Many of the students sitting in that homeroom rolled their eyes and snickered, knowing that the slick Lefky was about to unleash one of his most entertaining explanations for his tardiness. "Ms. Pellington," Lefkowitz began sincerely, "you know that I would never be late to your homeroom unless I had a very good reason. I was helping Mr. Costello with the trash, and I'm sure you know that he has not been in the best of health. Now how could I say no?"

Ms. Pellington is so very brand new to the school and unaware of the health status of the janitor or the well-known flim-flam artistry of Arthur Lefkowitz. "Well, Mr. Lefkowitz, I think your kindness to Mr. Costello is laudable and a credit to your character. Please just take your seat."

With that dazzling piece of palaver, some students were covering their mouths to stop from giggling as Lefkowitz had done it again, conning his way out of another jam.

Chapter 3

Carol Saphora

The sounds of teaching and learning at the high school begin to wane with the onset of seventh period, the last class of the day. The anticipation of the daily cessation of teacher voices, each with a distinctive voice, the muted banter filling the hallways, the tapping of leather-soled shoes, walking on the metal floors, and the chatter within each classroom builds to a cacophony as each door swings open with the booming of the dismissal bell at 2:15 p.m.

For junior John Kellin, the end of the school day carries an extra level of anticipation. John has always been a high-performing student, and no teacher or fellow student has a single memory of any grade John received in any class ever being anything other than an A. Ranked first in his class, beginning the junior year, this robustly built young man of six-foot, 190 pounds, is deceiving in appearance as he looks as though he could be a member of any of the high school athletic teams. However, John has no athletic inclination whatsoever. To his teachers, John is a delight to have in class, always first to volunteer answers to teacher-posed questions of fact and consequence.

John lives on Main Street in a lavish three-story gilded age home, the only son of Margaret and Conrad Kellin, a vice president of the Wallace Chemical Company, that enormous factory with the four billowing smokestacks on Quinnipiac Street.

6

Since ninth grade, John has had but one reoccurring distraction in life, a self-inflicted diversion that haunts his heart. On this fall afternoon, awaiting the bell for dismissal, John Kellin anticipates his distraction.

The bold sound of the afternoon bell finally sounds, and John leaves his Latin 3 classroom without a word to anyone. With all haste, he navigates the crowded hall to his locker, number B-24. John stands perpendicular to his locker, refraining from turning the dial on the combination lock that would open the tan metal door, keeping an eye focused across the corridor to the row of lockers on the other side of the hallway.

Trying to maneuver his head and eyes through the end-of-school student traffic in the hallway, the passing crowd began to dissipate, and suddenly, standing in front of locker B-56 was a girl who quickened his breathing and caused John to raise his chin, slightly lifting his head so the female in question might subjugate all his senses.

The object of his attention was Carol Saphora, who had just turned to her right to acknowledge another young man whose locker was next to hers. The flash of her smile required John to take a quick gulp of air through his nose, inhaling with a shuttering snuffle. John's mouth bloomed into a smile, and his lips parted to inhale enough air to sustain him.

Before him, in front of locker B-56, was junior Carol Saphora. Standing five-five with blue eyes and blond hair that framed her flawless face, she seemed to beam sunshine. She was the most beautiful girl John had ever seen, a conviction he held tight to since first seeing her when they were ninth graders.

As they stood across each other with the corridor of passing pupils between them, John caught Carol's eye, and she casually waved a little finger wiggle "hello." Even that insouciant gesture thrilled John, the fact that Carol acknowledged him. He looked forward to this fleeting moment every day and any other chance of sighting Carol before, during, or after school.

With all of John's confident demeanor, demonstrated in every class and extracurricular school activity, including serving as the current student council president, John would rarely muster enough courage to say more than a passing hello to Carol.

Just as John Kellin held a major-league crush on Carol, many other boys must have been infatuated with the appeal of Carol. On the other hand, Carol was gregarious and thoroughly enjoyed the repartee with other students. In a general interpretation of the expression "birds of a feather," Carol was usually in the company of the prettiest girls in the school when she wasn't shoulder to shoulder with Robert.

For all her popularity and unmistakable charm, Carol only had eyes for only Robert Ragsdale, another junior who was an apparent perfect fit for Carol. Tall (six-one) and strikingly handsome with a chiseled body, Bobby, to family and most friends, had short dark hair and brown eyes. The Ragsdale family lived on Main in a majestic seven-bedroom home with a stately second-story balcony at the front. Robert was the only son with two elder sisters.

The Ragsdales are of the most well-to-do families in Wallingford and give the most lavish parties. Robert is always well-dressed in school, wearing a navy blue blazer most of the time with what appears to be an embroidered family crest on the front pocket. The only faux pax in his appearance is his propensity to wear white athletic socks with his cordovan or black loafers, which most boys in high school seemed to wear.

Chapter 4

Julia

One of Main Street's endearing comfy cozy aspects is how the sidewalks become a haven for residents walking their dogs at dusk. Each day, no matter the weather or extreme degrees of temperature, the denizens of Main Street and the adjacent avenues leave their homes to walk their dogs.

From Mr. Elyward's pair of rescued greyhounds, Ace and Alice, to Dr. Ferguson's golden retriever, Queenie, and Ms. Yarbrough's Afghan hound, Dobee, the pavements bordering Main Street are a dog lover's paradise as the sun begins to set.

It is always entertaining how many of these dogs somehow resemble their owners. Mr. Elyward is a tall angular gentleman whose manner of walking has been described as an unfolding beach chair. His greyhounds are high-crotched and thin-legged. By the breed's nature, Ms. Yarbrough's Afghan possesses a long silky light-colored coat, while Yarborough dons blond tresses that reach the small of her back.

However, one dog and owner require a second glance from anyone walking or driving by. The young lady of the twosome is Julia Derigg, a junior at the high school. She is a lovely girl of sixteen with large hazel eyes and silkened brunet shoulder-length hair. At five-foot-five inches tall and just under a hundred pounds, she might appear not strong enough to handle any dog by a single strand of leash, but Julia and her companion have more than a loving friendship.

Her dog is a Shetland sheepdog named GaaGoo, a compelling aspect in the life of Julia.

9

Julia was a stunningly pretty girl, possessing an angelic face with glistening hair that she kept straight and long. A petite fifteen-year-old beauty, she held a short leash on GaaGoo as he sometimes would react to a passing car. Since her dog was a seven-month-old puppy, Julia would walk him down the sidewalk of North Main Street, almost to the middle of town. By the nature of its breed, a Sheltie is a herding dog and instinctively tended to "round things up," but Julia kept him close with his teal and gold collar and matching leash.

Julia's stride when walking was something of a strolling symphony, each step balanced. There were no hip-raking arm movements, which so many females included in their walk, just a consistent gait, almost floating. GaaGoo was always at her right side, and neither companion required a pull nor a yank of the leash.

Walking side by side, GaaGoo's soft eyes would continually look up at Julia as they strolled, a manner of communication of their own without sound.

As they walked together each day in one of the afternoon's later hours, they passed other dogs and their owners, but GaaGoo ignored the baying, barking, and occasional rearing up of other dogs. A squirrel might dart by, but GaaGoo would not react. His whole attention was on Julia. People would peer out of the windows of their Main Street homes or the Sweet Shop, where the high school kids gathered after school, or out the windows of the restaurant on the first floor of the opera house, watching Julia and her GaaGoo walk along. No observer failed to smile at the moving picture that was pretty Julia and her companion walking.

Julia caused people to wonder. Some students from the high school had seen her in the hallways, some even knew her name, but few, if any, knew much about her. One casual glance when Julia entered one's sight immediately posed questions in their thoughts. Julia is a story unto herself, somewhat mysterious, another tingle and tune in Main Street's forever vibration.

So who is this quiet, seemingly isolated beauty with a dog to match? To begin, Julia is the daughter of Scott and Emma, two incredibly devoted parents, whom doctors and specialists informed that their daughter Julia was born mute. Still unable to speak as a high school student, her loving parents have committed much of their lives to finding a solution to her lack of voice, taking her to doctors and language pathologists all over the country.

Julia has been medically identified as a "late-talker," and her family members and most speech pathologists believe that Julia will one day talk. Julia possesses the ability to hear and understands the speech of others. Julia began learning to "sign," a system of communication using visual gestures and signs, at eight months old, and with the help of an aide and the inspiration of her grandmother, Denise, who has devoted herself to the development of the child, Julia has earned high academic honors at every grade level.

Early in her life, doctors alerted her parents that Julia's inability to speak might be an indication of autism or dysarthria. Speech therapists worked to improve her breath support and used oral-motor exercises, but nothing would make the sounds of speech come forth from her mouth. As a toddler, she made an occasional mumbling sound of sorts but only when prompted to do so by a speech therapist, her mother, or her grandmother. Unfortunately, Julia never initiated her sounds for any reason, choosing to sign or tug at someone's garment for attention.

Both parents believed that music might serve as a catalyst for Julia to make sounds, leading to speech. Emma, Julia's mother, had played the piano since her youth. When Scott and Emma moved into their Main Street home, Emma believed that a piano was necessary for their elegant home.

On their second wedding anniversary, Scott bought his wife a baby grand piano that would become the centerpiece of the Victorian room on the eastern side of the house. The room featured curved arch windows with floor-to-ceiling white drapes. A Victorian chandelier of brass and crystal hung from the center of the ceiling, with mural wallpaper decorating the distinctive walls. The black Steinway baby grand was positioned on a circular Sarouk oriental rug at the room's center with the room's windows, behind the piano seat, providing natural light to the music.

At this Steinway, Emma provided her daughter with her first piano instruction. Julia instantly became enthralled by the piano and how pressing keys combined in endless cords and sound. By six, the young beauty would spend many hours each day at the piano with GaaGoo sitting by her side. Such was the rapid development of her piano skills that her parents brought in a recognized piano pedagogue to provide private lessons. Although Julia demonstrated some talent at the piano and enjoyed her time at the keyboard, her parents hoped that this might spark something within her and bring forth speech. Alas, words from her mouth did not emerge.

In the elementary grades, Julia developed reading skills far above her grade level and, at age eight, began to read the classics as her grandmother, Denise, who had learned to sign, would sit with her for hours. Denise watched the child's facial gestures for expressions of emotion and engagement in each book. They would read together, Julia in silence and Denise out loud. The brilliantly intellectual grandmother would softly explain concepts of love, anger, and fear contained in the reading, always with the hope that one day Julia would begin to talk with her.

At the age of nine years old, with the encouragement of her speech pathologists, Julia was able to make a grunting sound, but hearing herself was distasteful for her. Sometimes after making a grunting sound, Julia would shake her head back and forth as if to signal "no, no, no."

When around students and teachers, she purposefully shut down any sounds that might come from her mouth as these gruntings embarrassed her. Julia so wanted to say words more than anything. She prayed each night that God would let her talk, to converse with others, but she feared being mocked. In school, she often witnessed other students pointing at her and snickering as if they were saying, "Look at the mute kid." The dread of being laughed at pushed her more into silence. Julia was resolved to sign or write phrases to others on a five-by-seven pad she always carried with her.

Her grandmother tried to explain to Julia the meanness that some people sometimes display to others and stressed that she should look for the best in every person, no matter the bad things they might do. This lesson would not be lost on Julia as the years passed.

Julia's parents observed an intensity of concentration in the little girl. Julia was never distracted and meticulously prepared her assignments when reading or doing her homework. Most astonishing of all was Julia's ability to understand mathematical concepts. By junior high school, Julia was the highest-performing math student, illustrating her solutions to math problems on the blackboard with great detail but still unable to speak.

The continuous efforts of her parents to find some doctor, therapist, or agency that would, at long last, help Julia to speak led to a consultation with Dr. Henry Wharton in Boston when Julia was twelve years old. As requested by Dr. Wharton, Julia's parents, grandmother, therapists, and teachers completed extensive questionnaires about Julia that were submitted to the doctor for careful analysis. The beautiful teenager submitted to a long battery of tests over two days. One of Julia's exams was an intelligence quotient test that measured her cognitive capacity relative to her peer/age group. Julia's IQ was calculated as 142.

At the end of the evaluation, Dr. Wharton concluded that Julia demonstrated all the characteristics of the Einstein syndrome, a condition where a child experiences late-talking or a *late language emergence* but demonstrates extraordinary abilities in analytical thinking. According to Dr. Wharton, a child with Einstein syndrome would eventually speak but, in his professional opinion, would need a spark, a catalyst of sorts, to trigger speech.

The lengthy discussion with Dr. Wharton and his staff urged Julia's parents to provide a variety of stimulation for their little girl, including music, social activities, and maybe a pet. On the drive home from Boston, Emma, her mother, asked her daughter if she would like a pet of some kind. Julia immediately signed the letters "d-o-g" to her mother.

A month later, Julia traveled downstate to a dog breeder of Shetland sheepdogs (Sheltie). After talking about various breeds, Julia and her parents fell in love with the idea of purchasing a Sheltie puppy. This particular breed was so attractive to Julia and her parents because Shelties are intelligent, affectionate, trainable, and playful. Most importantly, the dog's weight would probably not exceed twenty-five pounds, making it easier to handle for the ninety-five-pound Julia.

Her mom and dad hoped a dog might ignite a spark in Julia, bringing forth speech.

Chapter 5

Welcome, GaaGoo

The sable-coated Sheltie puppy was clutched in Julia's arms as they entered their home on Main Street. Emma watched her daughter with arms full of puppy and thought, *Will our home ever be the same again?*

After their marriage, Emma and Scott searched for the right home for them for two years and spared no effort in maintaining and improving the majesty of this house built in 1882. Their Edwardian abode featured wide hallways and many nontraditional windows of various sizes and shapes. Now with a puppy added to their family, Emma dared to imagine the havoc the little thing might bring to bear on many of the handcrafted pieces of furniture, especially the pedestal Picardy dining room table, her favorite piece. However, Emma rationalized that if the puppy becomes a fixture in Julia's life, helping her find her voice, no piece of wood, no matter how well-designed, would not be worth the sacrifice.

With the puppy yapping most of the evening, Julia never let him out of her sight and took the baby Sheltie out to pee and poop twice before she crawled into her bed. Mother Emma determined that the puppy would be crate-trained, which didn't agree with Julia, who assumed she could take the puppy to bed with her.

With the shrill bark of the puppy in its crate in the dining room in the background, mother and father trailed Julia up to her bedroom to say good night. Before turning out the lights, Emma asked her daughter, "What name will you give your puppy?"

Julia began to sign something in response, and then quickly shook her head no with a smile.

Emma and Scott kissed their daughter good night in their traditional way. Each parent kissed each eye of Julia, followed by a kiss on each cheek, and the bedside light was switched off. Her parents departed her corner bedroom, then down the winding staircase as the pup's barking appeared to grow louder. Leaving the puppy alone with just a lit corner lamp, the Sheltie dog was soon circled up in a fluffy blanket in his crate and fell fast asleep.

Julia awakened in the early dawn, now Sunday morning, to the sound of a crying, more of a howling puppy. Rushing down the winding staircase to the dining room, Julia found her father already holding the puppy in his hands, speaking softly to the little puffball. As Julia approached, her father repeated the question of an evening ago, "What are you going to call him?"

Once again, Julia shook her head, but her facial expression with pursed lips and squinting eyes told her dad that Julia was thinking about a name for the little guy.

Throughout the day, Julia and her young dog were inseparable. She sat on the floor of the hallways and kitchen, smiling, feeling the softness of his fur and the structure of his tiny body. Periodically, her parents would drop in to watch her and the pup interacting but kept their viewing brief so as not to deter the two from growing their initial relationship.

Late in the morning, Emma was in her office with the French doors to the room open and heard a grunting sound. Curious and somewhat afraid, Emma rushed into the ornate corridor outside her office to find Julia and the puppy sitting on the hardwood floor. Julia was patting the palms of her hands on the floor in front of the dog, who was playfully swiping at Julia's movements with his paws. The fascinated mother watched for a few seconds and then heard the grunting sounds again—coming from Julia's mouth. Instantly, Emma felt her pounding heart. Her daughter was making a responsive utterance to the puppy play.

Not knowing exactly how she should respond, the loving Emma got down on her knees next to Julia and her pup. Julia looked up at her mother as a broad smile overwhelmed her face as wetness filled Emma's eyes. Choking back the tears, Emma asked again, "What is his name?"

Julia opened her mouth just a bit as if to take a breath as she cupped the puppy in her hands and lifted the tiny dog to her mother. Emma just looked into her daughter's face and softly asked, "And who is this?"

Julia's chin quivered, her eyes widened, and she painstakingly grunted, "GaaGoo."

With that sound, that utterance, Emma threw her arms around Julia and sobbed.

Julia kept the pup in her hands between her mother's embrace and her.

Emma raised her hands, bracketing Julia's pretty face, and asked, "Is that his name?"

Julia slowly nodded as she looked down on the tiny dog of sable fur and labored to work the sound once more, "Gaaaaaa," and then a slight pause and moaned, "Goo."

The emotionally overcome mother took the puppy from her daughter's hands and whispered, "Nice the meet you, GaaGoo."

Instantly, Julia nodded and wrapped her arms around her mother's neck, would not let go.

For the first time in her life, Julia had initiated a sound on her own. She did not require the prompting of the therapists or her parents.

Yes, it was more a moan than a word, more a grunt than a discernable name, but it came from the heart to the mouth of Julia.

It was a small victory, to be sure. It would not immediately lead to a flood of words from Julia as this trickle of sound just uttered was just a beginning. A fire of passion would be required to unlock the gift of speech and talking, indeed a more incredible inspiration. Emma and Scott would celebrate this day and this moment many times in the years to come.

Chapter 6

The Essay

For the somewhat solitary Julia, who avoided most interaction with other students, the companionship with her dog, GaaGoo, was a dynamic relationship. GaaGoo always followed Julia around their spacious home, from a growing puppy to a full-grown Sheltie. Sitting with her as she read and did her homework, GaaGoo would look into her eyes, and she into his. As an eighth-grade language arts assignment, students in the class were charged to write an essay on the subject "My Best Friend." As part of the assignment, each student would be required to read their writing before the class. In developing the project, the teacher, Mrs. Davenport, overlooked or failed to consider the additional challenges this might present to her top-performing student, Julia, who was mute.

Although Mrs. Davenport assured Julia that no one would ever laugh, the teacher realized there was no guarantee that some students might not laugh and that Mrs. Davenport couldn't warn her students not to laugh as this alone would result in embarrassment for Julia. Consequently, Mrs. Davenport took Julia aside and told her that she wouldn't have to present her essay before the class. To this, Julia reared up and wrote on her pad, "I will read my essay, even if everyone laughs at me."

With two weeks to prepare, Julia began to write the paper "My Best Friend." The essay was to be about her dog, GaaGoo. After penning three pages on notebook paper, she stopped cold and reconsidered the assignment.

Knowing she had to stand before the class and read her essay, she thought, *Well, maybe I will sign before the class.*

Instantly, Julia dismissed that idea as the other students would not know signing and might make fun of her.

Julia was becoming uneasy with this project and unsure how to approach it. She needed her go-to person, asking her mother to call her grandmother, Denise, who always has the answers and the arms to hold her when she is troubled. The very presence of her grandmother made any problem a lot easier to confront.

Chapter 7

Denise to The Rescue

Julia met her grandmother at the terrace door and applied a bear hug to the magnificently beautiful Denise. Together, they signed in the parlor in front of the ornate fireplace. Julia explained the assignment and her intention to write about her best friend, her dog, GaaGoo, but the problem was not the writing—it was reading it before the class.

Julia told her grandmother that her teacher offered to excuse her from the oral portion of the assignment, but she did not want her teacher or anyone to treat her differently.

As Denise and Julia sat on the floor signing back and forth, the grandmother asked her granddaughter to teach her with her hands everything about GaaGoo. Julia cocked her head to the left and then looked over at GaaGoo, who was cuddled up on the oval rug under the cocktail table just to the left of them.

A warm grin came to Julia's mouth, and she raised her hands before her. With slow protracted movements of her fingers, hands, and arms, she defined the size and shape of the little dog's body as if to bring him to her in a loving embrace. Although GaaGoo was but a few feet away, Julia painted the features of the imaginary GaaGoo, moving her fingers in circles and strokes to illustrate the texture of his coat, the length of his tail, and the thin bones of his legs.

Denise watched in awe as her granddaughter harnessed every muscle in her arms, hands, and fingers to show the shape and loving impressions of GaaGoo.

Never pausing to seek acclimation from her grandmother, Julia cupped her little hands together and manipulated her fingers to reveal GaaGoo's face, detailing his eyes, nose, and ears with the tips of her fingers.

The most captivating part of Julia's hands-created explanation of GaaGoo to her grandmother began with Julia placing two fingers two inches from each of her eyes. Looking through her gestures directly at her grandmother, Julia made slow circular movements around her eyes. Then cupping her hands before her face to depict the tiny size of puppy GaaGoo many months ago, Julia once again pointed back at her eyes with both hands. This time Julia made even smaller circles, indicating her little dog's brown eyes. Parting her lips as though she wished she could speak, Julia pointed to her eyes with her index fingers and then pointed to her mouth. Pausing for a few seconds to look at her grandmother, hoping Denise would understand, Julia repeated the gesture, first pointing to her eyes and then to her mouth.

The loving grandmother knew in that instant what Julia was saying with her hands, and she didn't need sign language to more clearly articulate the meaning. Julia explained in the most loving manner that GaaGoo talked to her with his eyes.

Julia seemed detached from the world around her as she poured out her love for GaaGoo in her every gesticulation. Denise's eyes trickled tears down her face in adoration and admiration for her granddaughter's demonstration of love.

When Julia's actions were done, she signed to Denise, "Grandmother, how do I read my essay to the class without signing?"

Denise leaned into Julia, kissed her left cheek, and said, "Show the class how much you love GaaGoo. Show them like you just showed me. Julia, my dearest child, teach them how to love."

Chapter 8

Arcade of Angels

The vast forty-foot courtyard that leads from the front of the high school's majestic pillars to the sidewalk of Main Street is barren of people throughout most of the day. At 2:00 p.m., the courtyard becomes a sea of energy and youthful excitement, beginning with the final bell of dismissal chimes.

Principal McCain's second-floor office contains a large picture window that sits aloft, overlooking the courtyard. From this vantage point, Mr. McCain and anyone who might be so privileged to be standing or sitting in his office have a bird's eye view of all the students who mingle in the courtyard after school.

McCain has an affectionate name for the school's courtyard, "the Arcade of Angels." He attached this appellation to this patch of pavement in the front of the school as an extension of a term of endearment he uses to describe his students, "my angels." One might assume that most students would make their way home with all possible speed at the end of the school day. However, aside from the relatively small number of students who play on the seasonal athletic teams or those who work after school, the courtyard serves as a gathering site for socialization, every dimension of discourse, and the point of embarkation to the Sweet Shop, *the* place to be as young people free themselves from the trappings of the school day.

The Sweet Shop is destination no.1, where students wrap themselves around the music of the day, companionate in the drinking of cherry Cokes and ice cream floats, but it all begins with interactions on the courtyard.

It is a familiar colloquialism for students crossing paths with others in the hallways and classrooms to say, "See you on the courtyard." More than a casual meeting location, the courtyard is the epicenter for youthful spirits and generational memories.

On this once cobblestone, now cement pavement courtyard, graduating classes have gathered, the school's athletic teams pose for their annual photos on the stairs, and the rarest of school and town-wide social events. The courtyard is truly the town's event center.

Chapter 9

Courtyard Culture

Early in the school year, with the temperatures still hovering around seventy degrees, the after-school Arcade of Angels is a place for renewing acquaintances as the angels (students) mingle to see who has grown taller, more beautiful, or handsome, all growing closer to adulthood.

The dismissal chimes had sounded on this particular late September afternoon, and the vacant courtyard became replete with students who came together in small assemblages. Organically, students are drawn to like-minded circles. Friendships are fostered on the courtyard with younger students pulled toward older groups who engendered common interests, from hot music to fast cars, or the predominant appeal of generations, "interest in the opposite sex." A casual stroll through the coteries on the courtyard invariably includes earshots of repartees that include who likes who, who broke up with whom, or who has no chance with whom.

As like groups tend to swim together, three girls gathered on this day on the most southerly corner of the courtyard: Joey Galacious, Ingrid Canals, and Linda Rosens. Their voices, muffled by the din of the many conversations raging on in the throng, periodic stark comments emerged from the trio, such as "Stop, you're killing me," "No way," or a general guffaw as they traded comments and rhetorical questions, such as "And did you hear this ... ?"

Each of these girls is among the well-known set at the high school. Joey, a brunette, whose hair was long enough to wear it up in a perfectly circular bun, is a clothes maven as her mother has spoiled her, buying her the latest styles even before they hit the fashion magazines. She has eyes for many boys, but most of them are dating other girls. A gossip enthusiast, Joey would often begin a conversation with the demanding phrase, "Give me the dirt."

Ingrid is blonde, which doesn't begin to describe her luxurious hair color. Better described as auricomous, her hair has drawn the attention of nearly every male student. Some boys go so far as to volunteer to hand out materials in class so they may walk behind Ingrid as she sits in class and lay a not-so-accidental touch on the back of her over-the-shoulders locks.

Incredibly attractive with an exotic look that melts a boy with a wink of the eye or a raise of the eyebrow, Ingrid refers to her appearance approach as "working the look." Her darker eye makeup adds a dramatic allure as she sports long straight blond hair. Regardless of the season, Ingrid has an affinity for wearing black.

The third young lady in this triune is Linda, a highly introspective girl who finds the best in everyone and is quick to offer compliments. When she speaks to another student or adult, her eyes connect directly into the eyes of the recipient of her conversation. Linda oozes sincerity, making her one of the most genuine students in the school, and she makes everyone around her feel like the most special person in the world.

Amid the animated talking of the three young ladies, each girl had her eyes upon the landscape of students on the courtyard with its drone of diverse diatribe, laughter, and invectives. In the attribution of a typical early school year, there are new faces to discover, and each student enthusiastically dares to challenge the instantaneous feelings of the heart; vis-a-vis "who looks interesting," "who stimulates the metaphorical indicator of my 'like-meter,'" and "who suddenly turns me on."

Joey, Linda, and Ingrid spoke within their small circle, but each tarried to find a magnetic pull of drawn attention from a boy or boys from across the courtyard. To be sure, these three girls had no shortage of boys who would gladly demonstrate fealty for a single opportunity to go out on a date with one of them. Their conversation included random points of reference, such as "Hey, isn't that Charlie White? Doesn't he have the most dreamy eyes?" or "Take a gander at Barry Stubben. He looks soooo gooood."

With all the swirling repartee of the courtyard regarding all things related to the school and social interaction, on this crisp fall afternoon, a singular topic of buzz was embedded in most conversations, notably the annual First Lighting of the Lantern Gala. No student of the high school or denizen of this fair town was not aware of this glorious annual festival.

The Lantern

A striking appurtenance stands majestic in the western corner of the courtyard. It is a twelve-foot-high wooden pole with an iron hook affixed to its top, poised and sufficiently robust to hold a suspended pendulous lantern of tin and copper. Upon that hook, a lantern is hung, whose purpose and dynamic legacy are the source of community pride.

It is far more than a traditional fixture on the high school courtyard. Over time "the lantern" is a place of great sentiment and romantic moments for so many of the town faithful.

Girdled at its base with seasonal flowers maintained by the Brubaker family, the Lantern is a rallying place in the town, erected initially to only be lit when the high school's basketball team was victorious in an away contest, especially during the state basketball tournament.

Scores of townspeople who could not travel to the games would gather on the courtyard, beginning at 7:00 p.m. on away game nights, awaiting the Lantern to be lit by old Mr. Pattberg, who lived on Prince Street.

In the early rushes of the fall, local anthophiles, Egon and Edna Brudacker, plant and subsequently maintain chocolate cosmos (*Cosmos atrosanguineus*) in manicured circular rows around the wooden pole suspending the Lantern high above the courtyard.

No citizen of the fair town could not know of this annual tradition since 1931, but younger members of the student body, some new to our fair community, would sometimes inquire, "What is this legend of the Lantern?"

Chapter 10

The Sweet Shop

Students will invariably think about their plans for the after-school hours throughout the school day. While some will lament that they must get to an after-school job site to earn some much-needed bucks, others will trudge off to "practice" for one of the school athletic teams. Students who have fallen behind in a specific class might seek out a teacher for "extra help," while some will return home as quickly as possible to work on the family farm. Extracurricular activities that include organizational meetings and rehearsals keep the school alive with energy far after the formal end of the school day, but there is one after-school destination that makes most students joyful—the Sweet Shop.

The Sweet Shop is just a five-minute trot from the school, north on Main, taking a left on Center, just past Marvin's Shoes. As you approach the white storefront, you can hear the tunes of the jukebox coming through the brass-handled front door. It is always loud enough to be heard by passersby, albeit foot or car traffic.

Once inside, there are booths on both sides of the shop, flanking a glass-topped middle counter with fixed metal stools with round red leather seats. Behind the enclosed horseshoe-shaped middle counter are wooden tap handles that provide seltzer and Coca-Cola when pulled. Candy of various types is displayed for sale under the glass, from penny candy to the popular bars of Milky Way and 3 Musketeers, to the boxes or small bags Good & Plenty, Dots, M&M's, and an array of chewing gum brands that included Juicy Fruit, Bazooka, Chiclets, and Doublemint.

The Sweet Shop featured a variety of flavors of ice cream, floats, and milkshakes, almost anything sweet that would ruin someone's appetite for dinner at home.

When it came to the teenage crowd who noisily jammed in the door of the Sweet Shop after school, the drink of choice was a cherry Coke, a hand-stirred beverage in a tall glass of seltzer and some mixture of cherry syrup. The kids would guzzle cherry Cokes, and fifteen cents you could get a cherry Coke (ten cents) and a bag of potato chips (just a nickel).

The owner, Mr. Joe Connors, usually does the honors of mixing the drinks of cherry Coke one by one. Each person who comes into the Sweet Shop is greeted with a yelled-out, "Hi there!" by Mr. Connors as he never leaves the horseshoe of the counter.

To all the high school kids who frequent his place, he is known as Joe. He sees everyone who enters and knows many of his young customers on a first-name basis.

Upon entering, each customer, primarily teenagers, immediately will grab an empty booth, and if they don't find an unoccupied booth, they can sit at the counter or find someone they know who is sitting in a booth and ask them to "push in," cramming another person in a booth that is only meant to seat six, at best. Often the kids will sit on one another's lap in a booth, making what Mr. Connors describes as an attempt to put two pounds of baloney in a one-pound bag.

The Sweet Shop is a bustle of energy from 2:30 p.m. to 5:00 p.m. most weekdays and closes at 10:00 p.m. If there is a basketball game at the high school, the Sweet Shop is jammed to capacity after the game, and no one knows precisely how many people have been packed into the place at one time.

Mr. Connors enjoys the youthful energy and has been a great fan of the high school's basketball teams for many years, although he rarely has an opportunity to see a game at the high school. Pictures of past basketball teams decorate the walls of the Sweet Shop.

On game nights, Connors always keeps a booth of the Sweet Shop blocked out in reserve for members of the basketball team and cheerleaders after the game. Joe treats the players and cheerleaders like royalty. Such is the entrance of the team and cheerleaders that the patrons of the Sweet Shop applaud them loudly when they enter. Whether it is a marketing tactic or just an act of sentiment, it causes quite a stir when the team members show up at the front door.

The music from the jukebox, positioned at the back of the Sweet Shop, is played loud as Mr. Connors keeps it cranked up from some control knob at the back of the jukebox. Almost all the booths at the Sweet Shop have a little jukebox. For a quarter, you get three song choices. One of the problems is that you have to wait for everyone who puts in a quarter ahead of you to get their songs played. Sometimes a bunch of girls at a booth will keep playing the same song over and over. Even though Joe changes the records in the master jukebox to include the latest hit songs, he still leaves oldie records in the system, and they get played constantly. After all, how many times can you hear "I Only Have Eyes for You" by the Flamingos or "Mack the Knife" by Bobby Darin?

Arthur "Lekfy" Lefkowitz is more than a favorite patron of the Sweet Shop. Students come to the shop and try to get a booth near Lefky as there is always so much activity and nonsensical craziness all around him. An extra-large booth is just to the right of the jukebox, and it too is reserved for a particular group or, more specifically, one person and his circle of confederates known as his tribe. Mr. Connors treats Lefky with an extra-special congeniality. He will often sit with Lefky and his tribe and share the frivolity of the group.

Among his many peculiarities, Lefky liked to call almost everyone—boys, girls, and teachers—by a nickname he concocted. Most students were flattered by Lefky's handles, and others found them offensive. Faculty members didn't know of Lefky's nicknames for them unless a teacher saw it scribbled on a desk or some corner of a restroom wall. At the Sweet Shop, Lefky would often go from booth to booth and assign a nickname to students seated there.

The three guys who ran with Lefky had well-known nicknames: Gerald Banderino was Bando, George Owelowski was Owl, and Arsenella Holcomb was Arse. Together, Bando, Owl, and Arse followed their outspoken leader, Lefky, and often dared to get into trouble at his behest.

Chapter 11

Loomis and The Lantern of Love

Principal McCain believed in the value of monthly "assembly programs" in the auditorium. For the September assembly program for the freshly minted sophomore class, the youngest of the three classes at the high school, McCain decided to focus the forty-five-minute assembly on the history of the school and its cherished Lantern legend.

The main speaker for this oration was the always vivacious Mrs. Hildagaard Loomis, a graduate of the class of 1927 and a social studies teacher at the high school. She was one of the most popular teachers at the high school as her classes were, if nothing else, always entertaining. When she gave her classes quizzes and exams, her essay questions allowed students to express their opinions rather than the simple regurgitation of historical facts. As quirky and engaging as Mrs. Loomis appeared to be each day before her social studies students, she knew her local history cold and was fervent in her recreation of moments worthy of remembrance.

Mrs. Loomis approached the school's historic podium at center stage of the auditorium, facing the assembled students of the sophomore class precisely on schedule at 9:30 a.m. Fittingly, Mrs. Loomis stood behind the extraordinary antique French walnut wood podium, which was a gift from the visiting French ambassador following his visit to the high school in 1936. The same auditorium where he witnessed the senior class play, an adaptation of the French play *No Exit* by Jean Paul Sartare. This magnificent lectern, used in every graduation ceremony and memorable celebration, is a rare Gothic Revival piece of furniture, architecturally shaped with columns and broken arches.

The podium was built in the form of a pentagon made up of wooden planks, with each panel molded with columns carved in the round and arches, while the base has its extensive stepped moldings. Theoretically, the wide countertop and single shelf below are large enough to fit two people tucked into a captive embrace.

Mrs. Loomis, with her distinctive booming voice that is never one to be ignored, began her comments with an introduction of the historic opening of the high school in 1916 as a seminal moment for the town of Wallingford. She stated that the new building had a state-of-the-art auditorium, manual skills shop areas, science classrooms, and a gymnasium with the capability of conversion into a banquet hall for proms and seasonal dances.

Mrs. Loomis explained that the new high school instantly became the community's mecca for the most significant town events. Concerts, plays, and large town functions were held throughout the calendar year, but the events that drew the largest audiences were basketball games, where the local high school team played some of the best high school teams from across the state.

Early in the school's history, the basketball teams won six consecutive league championships, from 1927-28 to 1932-33. By the beginning of the 1930s, all home basketball games were standing room only, made all the more unique by the asymmetrical design of the gym with baskets flatly affixed to the north and south walls.

However, there was a problem for Wallingford citizens. As they loved their high school's basketball teams, traveling to away games was challenging in terms of distance, the unpredictable weather of New England, and the probability of getting lost. The high school team played away contests in every far corner of the state, requiring the use of state atlas maps that detailed intricate maneuvering of back roads and byways. An interstate highway system had yet to be constructed or even envisioned in the 1930s, so the intuitive utilization of the paper maps, augmented by a pocket compass, was often required. There were no Global Positioning System (GPS) units to guide one's path, and the only communications technology available was the telephone, a "ma-bell" dial device housed in a glass-doored booth, usually erected on a busy intersection.

The people of Wallingford figuratively lived and died on the outcome of the high school's basketball games. The high school basketball team was Wallingford's team.

When the team was playing an away game, Wallingford citizens, not to mention the current students, would call the police department and the school's principal at his home at all hours of the night to inquire about the score of each game. People couldn't seem to get off to sleep on the night of away games without knowing the game's outcome.

By 1930, the principal had become annoyed by the seemingly endless telephone calls to his home inquiring about the night's away basketball game results. The Wallingford citizenry literally hung on the outcome of every game, home and away.

High school basketball was almost a winter religion for the people of Wallingford. Although there were those who followed the basketball team vehicle, an orange-painted wood-paneled station wagon, that transported the team and coach, there were no buses to carry the team or students when it traveled to away locations for these games. The citizenry waited for game results like Christmas presents.

So the throngs of Wallingford citizens and students had to wait for game results long into the evening after a game had been completed or wait until morning. Several strategies were tried, but finally, the principal arrived at a workable idea. In 1931, he arranged to have a candle street lantern affixed to a ten-foot wooden pole erected in the western corner of the school's courtyard. When the coach called him after a victory, the principal would alert a resident of Wallingford who lived on nearby Prince Street, one Orville Pattberg, a cabinet-maker by trade and a faithful loyalist of all things Wallingford. Once called by the principal that the boys had indeed won the evening's basketball game, Orville would carry his small folding ladder to the courtyard and, subsequently, light a six-foot-long torch used to ignite the Lantern's six-inch-thick white candle affixed to an iron hook at the top of the pole.

As the courtyard is relatively dark at night, with only the headlights of intermittent passing cars to spread minimal illumination onto Main Street and the front of the high school. The lit candle of the Lantern was made more reflective by the highly polished metals inside of the Lantern that gave off a vibrant aura of sunburst shades of red and burned orange.

Mrs. Loomis painted the verbal picture that, since 1931, large crowds would gather on the high school courtyard on the nights of away basketball games to watch for the lighting of the Lantern, signaling a victory. One of the largest reported crowds gathered in 1937 as approximately five hundred persons huddled in a falling snowstorm for hours to see if the Lantern would burn on the occasion of the state basketball final game.

Mrs. Loomis took a deep breath and altered the tenor and tone of her words. Now all school history and those big game moments are all well and good and worthy of celebration, but there is far more to the legend of the Lantern than the bounce of a basketball or the fleeting moments of an athletic event.

The First Lighting of the Lantern Gala is an extravagant outdoor celebration patterned after the annual royal ball of Wallingford, England, the town's namesake, brought forward to this country when the town was established in 1670. Softening her voice and momentarily peering upward toward the patterned filagree of the hand-painted ceiling above the stage, her face had a haze of sentimentality, explaining in a slow and protracted manner.

The recreation of the centuries-old British formal ball was purposefully brought to life by the planners of the First Lighting of the Lantern Gala in 1932.

Maintained in all its pristine splendor in early November of each year, the First Lighting of the Lantern Gala is a beautiful confluence of the ancient, the time-revered, and most importantly, the beautiful moments of love and sentiment that remain forever in every young girl's dreams.

Mrs. Loomis's last few comments garnered the attention of every student in the assembly as these words spoke to an unspoken yet long-wished-for desire of every heart, old and young. Mrs. Loomis looked out from her perch behind the majestic podium as if to peer into every student's eyes simultaneously, unveiling the most powerful attribute of the legend of the Lantern. Mrs. Loomis edified, "As with every legend, a prophecy is attached. It is rarely spoken aloud, for if even the echoes of the words of the prophecy are heard, they might disappear like a puff of smoke into the night."

A sophomore girl of brunet hair and brown eyes seated in the second row, hanging on every word of Mrs. Loomis's tale of legend and love, called out, "Tell us, what is this prophecy all about?"

Motioning the student to rise from her seat, Mrs. Loomis lifted her hands before herself as if to catch a sprinkling of the innocence of this student. She avers, "For this young lady and all of you hearing the sound of my voice, the legend of the Lantern states, 'If first kissed under the lantern, your heart shall be moonlit forever after.'"

Chapter 12

The Algebra Stare

Recognized by teachers and students alike as the most demanding teacher in the school was Mr. Arnold Crampitz, a stodgy mathematics teacher in his sixties who delivered instruction in traditional math teacher mode with his back to the class. He would write on the blackboard and talk simultaneously, leaving his students to see the wrinkles on the backside of his sports jacket. Demanding and condescending, he often would ask a question of his students, and before a student would come to the blackboard to write a solution, he would write in large letters, "2 E Z." Mr. Crampitz certainly knew his subject well but found it difficult to understand how any student could not comprehend the concepts he taught in Algebra II.

As Mr. Crampitz was the only teacher in the school who taught Algebra II, any student who had plans on taking the full complement of math classes necessary for the best preparation for the SAT and the subsequent matriculation to a four-year university had to endure a full-year course with Mr. Crampitz. Many students labeled his classroom 218 as the torture chamber.

There were two sections of Algebra II class; one was scheduled in the morning and one in the afternoon. Although students had no say in which section they were enrolled as it was contingent on what other subjects a student was taking, most agreed that it was best to be in the morning Algebra II class with Mr. Crampitz. The morning hours were a time of day when a student was fresh and before Mr. Crampitz could get cranky after lunch.

The morning class had fifteen students, including junior class "brains" John Kellin, Francine Riale, Andrew Kapinski, and Julia Derigg. Among these high achievers were eleven other students who demonstrated varying analytical skills. As ever, Mr. Crampitz catered his instruction to the fast-moving mathematical minds rather than those who needed a more patient measured approach to teaching. He expected every student to keep up, and consequently, some students opted to transfer to other less challenging classes, such as "The Yo-Yo as an Art Form."

For most teachers, one of the telltale signs that teaching a concept, theory, or fact has taken seed in students is the body language exhibited by the seated learners. That observable teacher tool also works in reverse when a student looks confused or just plain dumbfounded. For Mr. Crampitz, who rarely turned around from writing on the blackboard, when he did look back over his students, he would witness some nodding heads in acknowledgment that there was understanding.

Then there was the inevitable look of a student who stared back at him, seemingly looking up through their eyebrows with a gaping open mouth, appearing to be in a state of confusion. For Mr. Crampitz, this was known as the algebra stare, a sure signal of mathematical bewilderment.

Mr. Crampitz had written a partial equation on the blackboard and speaking in his typical sarcastic manner, said to the class, "I want one of you to come to the board and attempt to solve the quadratic."

With that request, only John Kellen and Julia Derigg raised their hands. Mr. Crampitz ignored his two prized students' hands and looked around the room for an unsuspecting student, one who exhibited a clear algebra stare. The veteran teacher found one right away and zeroed in on a student who had not fared well on any of his recent quizzes and tests. Mr. Crampitz called out, "Robert (Ragsdale), suppose you come forward ... Factor and solve the quadratic."

Robert was looking down, his face buried in his math textbook, trying not to be noticed. When he heard the gristle voice of Mr. Crampitz calling his name, he knew he was doomed. Exposing himself to his teacher's wrath, Robert arose from his chair and sheepishly confessed, "Mr. Crampitz, I don't understand how to factor."

Ragsdale was clearly embarrassed, an emotion not lost on Julia Derigg, who felt terrible for the tall handsome boy in the back row.

A disgusted look came over Mr. Crampitz's face, and he resolved to move along in his lesson. He looked to the radiant girl in the front row. "Ms. Derigg, would *you* please come up here and demonstrate to Mr. Ragsdale and the rest of the class how we correctly factor and solve for the quadratic?"

Julia walked the few steps from her front-row desk to the blackboard, picked up a piece of chalk from the ledge, and completed the problem easily. As she returned to her seat, Mr. Crampitz directed a scathing rebuke to Robert, "You see how easy that was, Ragsdale? Do you think you might take time out from your athletic endeavors to study your math?"

With more than twenty minutes remaining in class, Mr. Crampitz assigned two problems to his students at the back of the chapter, on page 143. Not done with the befuddled Robert Ragsdale, Mr. Crampitz directed, "Ms. Derigg, I wonder if you would please go sit in the back of the room with Mr. Ragsdale and try to help him gain some appreciation for the quadratic and the process of factoring?"

Upon hearing Mr. Crampitz assign the *mute kid* to tutor him, Robert rolled his eyes and looked over at one of his football teammates in the class, John Ronzino, who was enjoying a laugh over the circumstances.

Julia moved herself to the open seat next to Robert and opened her math book to the chapter on factoring. Julia began by writing a series of numbers and algebraic expressions on a piece of paper in front of him.

Still embarrassed and obviously ticked off by Mr. Crampitz's actions, Robert did not look at Julia's writings or her. After a few minutes of Robert's despondency, Julia grabbed his right hand and abruptly placed it on the paper she had written. Instantly, Robert turned his head to look at Julia and found her glaring back at him. No smiles were forthcoming as Robert got the message that this little long-haired girl, who could not talk, was serious about her task, but there was something else. In grasping Robert's right hand, Julia saw and felt his fingers. They were long and slender, and the skin of his hand was smooth and free of any dryness, cuts, or abrasions.

Placing a pencil in his hand, Julia made numerical gestures with her fingers and then pointed to Robert, signaling that he try and solve the factoring exercise. Julia pointed to the first example in factoring with Robert's hand on the paper. Other students were watching, and Robert knew they were looking, adding to the moment's discomfort. Julia slowly maneuvered the pencil, writing the correct answer with her guiding their hands. When Robert wrote what he thought was a correct answer, Julia immediately made a parallel waving motion with her hand over the paper, which meant, "No, you are wrong."

The subtlety of her hand movements allowed Julia to correct Robert with nothing that would embarrass the young man. Now Julia once again placed her hand over Robert's, sharing the holding of the pencil.

Robert left himself in Julia's hand. He asked her questions as she wrote each figure with him. She would stop for a few seconds and looking into his face, would nod as if to say, "Are you getting this?"

Robert spoke in a quiet voice so only Julia could hear his questions. Sometimes she would write on her pad a specific question, such as "Robert, is this becoming clearer to you?"

Lo and behold, in those twenty minutes of tutoring, Robert was beginning to understand. It all seemed so obvious now to him, so easy. As Mr. Crampitz alerted his students that the bell for the end of class was about to ring, Robert turned to Julia with a smile and said, "Thank you."

She cocked her head, looking back at Robert, almost quizzically feeling a little something inside of her. As he got up to return to his regular seat, Julia grabbed his arm as if to indicate, "Wait a second." She wrote on her pad, "Robert, you can do math if you believe you can."

Ripping off the page from her pad, she handed it to Robert as the tall Ragsdale returned to his seat.

Putting the note in his math book, the bell rang, and everyone piled out of the classroom, except Julia. She waited until everyone else had departed and again felt something new in her. Mr. Crampitz spoke sarcastically to her as she headed for the door, "Julia, thanks for helping the *jock* count."

As she stepped into the hallway to walk to her next class, she caught a glimpse of Robert, who was walking and joking around with his friends. She watched him until he turned the corner and was out of sight. As Julia strode to her next class, chemistry, she experienced a unique feeling. She had a nervous stomach as though she had eaten something that didn't agree with her.

Once seated, Julia began to consider how really far behind Robert was in Algebra II. She didn't understand why she was so concerned about a boy, or anyone for that matter, who had probably neglected his study of the subject, but for some reason, she felt sorry for Robert. There was something else that produced in her some bewilderment. Julia kept thinking about Robert's thick dark hair that hung straight down over his forehead. She couldn't stop thinking about it, and then there was his hand with such long thin fingers. Julia was confused by her preoccupation with Robert.

Few students ever talked to Julia, and obviously, Julia could not speak to them. In the idle time, waiting for chem class to begin, Julia wrote, "Robert Ragsdale" on her five-by-seven pad for no apparent reason, without much forethought.

Seated next to her was Diane Deere, a cheerleader in Julia's homeroom throughout high school since their last names started with the letter D and because Diane was a good student who always seemed to show up in her classes. Diane casually looked around the classroom, smiling and chatting with other students. Giving in to being "nosey," Diane looked over at Julia's desk and the notepad with the handwritten name, "Robert Ragsdale."

Diane instantly recognized the name belonging to the popular good-looking basketball team member, who was the apple of Carol Saphora's eye, a fellow cheerleader. Diane wondered why Julia, of all people, would write his name on her pad.

Although she had hardly ever said hello to Julia before, Diane leaned closer to Julia and pointing to the name on her pad, asked, "Oh, you know Bobby Ragsdale?"

Instantly, Julia felt embarrassed, as if she had no right to write his name, and shook her head back and forth to indicate no.

Diane sensed Julia's discomfort, apologetically saying, "Sorry ... I was being a busybody." Diane saw Julia's face become flushed and tried to ease her reserved classmate's momentary rush of reaction, commenting, "Bobby is a great kid, nice eyes, don't you think?"

This was the first time Julia ever shared a conversation with Diane, even though they had known each other throughout their public school years. Julia had always admired Diane, who was always stylishly dressed, possessing a wonderful smile. Diane lived along North Main Street, and Julia would sometimes see her sitting on her front porch when she walked GaaGoo. Now maybe Julia would wave to Diane on her walks. Julia thought, *Wouldn't it be nice to have Diane as a friend?*

As chemistry class came to an end, Diane touched Julia's desk as if to say goodbye, something that other students never gestured or said to her.

Stepping into the hallway flow, Julia looked left and right. Maybe Robert might be passing by.

Chapter 13

Helping Robert

As Julia dined with her parents, completed homework, and practiced her piano, her thoughts were of Robert Ragsdale all through the evening. Julia naturally possessed laser focus on any assignment or task, but the hovering distraction concerning Robert Ragsdale was disarming and oh so new.

She wished she could share her thoughts with someone more than ever before, and she wanted to express her feelings. Something was very different inside of her, and she wished her mother or grandmother were there to understand her feelings without saying words.

Before bedtime, Julia sat with her dog, GaaGoo, looking into his eyes. She wondered, *Does GaaGoo know how I feel now?*

The next day Julia anticipated math class with a bit of added zing. As she arrived at the door of 218, someone grabbed Julia's left arm and lightly pulled her to the middle of the hallway. Upon seeing that Robert had grabbed her arm, she took an instant short breath and dropped the two books she was carrying. Robert immediately knelt to pick up her books and papers and handed them back to Julia; he noticed his girlfriend, Carol Saphora, glaring at him from the bunch of students walking in the other direction.

With her books restored to her hands, Robert looked into her face and quietly pleaded, "What can I do? I am totally lost in math the last few weeks."

Julia's face showed great empathy, or was it something else her face revealed as she looked up at the tall Ragsdale? At that moment, Mr. Crampitz stepped into the doorway of 218 and urged students to make an immediate entry.

Julia didn't have time to respond to Robert as the students found their seats, with Julia seated front desk center. As Mr. Crampitz assumed his teaching position at the front of the room, facing the blackboard, Julia hurriedly came up with a plan to assist Robert, writing a note to be given to Robert on her pad. "Robert, we are on the same lunch wave. I'll help you with your math at lunch. Go to the corner table near the trash cans. I'll meet you there."

At the end of math class, Julia gave the once-folded note to Robert and got along to chemistry class, not waiting for a reply, just assuming he was serious about getting help in Algebra II.

The next day, as Robert walked with Carol to the cafeteria, he explained that he would not be sitting with her and "the gang," his teammates and their friends. When Robert told Carol he was getting help from Julia, the possessive Carol nastily retorted, "You're getting help from the kid who can't even talk?"

Robert came to Julia's defense. "She is bright and is the best Algebra II student in old Mr. Crampitz's class. If she can't teach me, no one can."

It didn't escape Carol's notice that Julia was a lovely girl despite her inability to speak, and jealousy was smoking.

CHAPTER 14

The Tutoring Begins

Julia sat with Robert at lunch and drilled him without pause or mercy in the processes and skills necessary to pass Algebra II. Julia used every means possible to instruct Robert but was certainly slowed by her inability to speak. Every bit of instruction had to be written on her pad for Robert to read. As she did in their first help session during class, Julia would often place her hand on Robert's, and together, they would move the pencil in solving problems.

Although Carol Saphora was seated in the middle of the cafeteria, a relative distance from the corner table where Robert and Julia were seated, Carol kept a sharp eye on the two of them. Although Robert was trying to stay focused on his math tutoring, he would often raise his head and look over at the table where Carol sat with her friends and fellow cheerleaders. Every time he would look over, Carol was glaring back at him.

As Julia discovered, people, especially immature high school students, will sometimes be cruel. As tuned in as she was to tutoring Robert, Julia's keen hearing made her privy to some of the sarcastic comments emanating from neighboring tables, but nothing would break her focus on helping him.

After the first week of Julia's tutoring, Mr. Crampitz sprung a surprise quiz on his Algebra II classes. While writing out the problems to be solved on the blackboard, Mr. Crampitz remarked, "Ragsdale, I understand that little Julia here has been giving you some extra help.

I want to let you know that effort alone will get you nowhere with me. You need to pass this quiz and get at least a B on the end-of-quarter examination in two weeks to pass this course. By the way, Mr. Ragsdale, this quiz is dirt-simple ... even for you."

Whereas some school-spirited teachers might give a star athlete, like Robert, a break in the way of an extra-credit assignment or extra time on an examination, Mr. Crampitz was of no such inclination.

Julia, who never found reason to be angry, was furious with Mr. Crampitz for how he was talking to Robert. At that moment, Julia wished she could speak so that she might rebuke Mr. Crampitz for his meanness, but she was confined to her inner feelings without verbal expression.

Julia was confident that Robert would pass the quiz after her first week of helping him, or so she hoped. The other outcome of that week of lunchtime math lessons was that Julia realized just how far behind Robert was in math.

While Julia had always enjoyed everything about math, Robert treated math as a chore and got no joy out of understanding and solving problems.

CHAPTER 15

Heart and Hands

After a week of tutoring Robert, Julia's thoughts were unaccustomedly scattered on leaving the school on that Friday afternoon. Usually, when the school day was over, she would walk home along Main Street, anticipating seeing her GaaGoo and doing her homework with the adorable dog by her side. Today her attention was easily distracted. She noticed people holding hands, particularly Diane Deere, who had been so kind to her a few days ago and was holding the hand of another junior class member, David Cadwalader. David was Julia's partner on a science project in sixth grade. He was of medium height and had auburn hair and blue eyes. Julia watched the couple saunter, occasionally laughing, strolling down Main and wondered how holding a boy's hand felt. Then it occurred to Julia. Her hand and Robert's were touching as she tutored him. Quickly dismissing that touching as anything other than math help, Julia's thoughts turned to Robert's hand. His hand had such long thin fingers. *This is crazy*, she thought. *Why am I thinking of this boy's hand?*

Diane noticed Julia walking on the other side of Main Street and waved at her, calling out, "Julia, are you going to the Sweet Shop"?

Julia had often passed the after-school soda shop but had never been inside the teenage gathering place, nor had anyone ever asked her to go there. Shaking her head no, she smiled and continued her walk home.

As she crossed Center Street and passed the "old well" used to water horses in the late nineteenth century, her thinking turned to how she could help Robert pass Algebra II. During one of their lunch-wave sessions, she asked him if he wanted to work on math after school, but Robert told her that he had team practice after school.

Somehow Julia felt responsible for Robert. She didn't know why. It didn't make much sense. She thought, *If Robert doesn't want to sacrifice a few silly sports practices so he can pass Algebra II, why should I care?*

Upon arriving home, Julia was pleased to see her grandmother's car parked in the driveway.

Grandmother Denise stood in the foyer as Julia opened the wide mahogany door with dual stained glass windows by the polished brass door handle.

Julia threw her arms around her grandmother and led her into the sitting room opposite the piano room. Julia began to "sign" frantically to Denise, her grandmother, who saw her granddaughter's urgency and asked her to please slow down.

Julia explained that her math teacher had asked her to help this boy named Robert Ragsdale, who was dreadfully behind. As Julia signed her way through the details of the first in-class help she gave Robert to the just completed week of math-help meetings during lunch each day, Denise watched her eyes and began to smile. The gentle and demure grandmother sensed that something sweet was brewing inside Julia. When her granddaughter ended the frenzied hand language, Denise quietly inquired, "So what do you like about this Robert Ragsdale?"

The question caught Julia off guard as she responded in sign, "Well, Grandma, he's tall and ..."

Julia quickly stopped signing, gathered herself, and wrote on her pad, "I don't like him. I am just helping him pass Algebra II."

Tilting her head back, letting out a smiling giggle, Denise looked into the face of her cherished grandchild and commented, "Oh, so you don't like Robert, huh? That must mean you are forced to help him or you just feel sorry for the lad."

Julia knew in a second that her grandmother had figured something out that she had yet to understand or accept.

Denise reached out as if to hug her and looking into her eyes, said, "It's all right," and touching Julia's upper left shoulder, "your heart does not have an off and on switch. Your heart will feel what it feels ... bring you joy in feeling ... and sometimes love rains down upon you."

Julia was now somewhat defensive as this back-and-forth was too serious, too uncomfortable.

The loving grandmother, Denise, knew there was more to this scenario than just a noble effort to help another student with math difficulties. Denise got quiet for a few moments and looking into her granddaughter's eyes, asked, "Julia? You really like this boy, don't you"?

Julia looked away from her grandmother and began to cry.

Denise sensed something else. There was more to this than a girl's first crush. This was a brilliant young lady who, by no fault of her own, was forced to live in a relative social cocoon during her young life. Whatever Julia felt about people or things she had seen with her eyes or heard with her ears, she kept them bottled up inside of her. It was apparent to Denise that Julia might have real feelings for this boy named Robert.

It was all very natural and predictable for a teenage girl, but for Julia, who could not vent the vibrations of her heart with her voice, the potential for emotional upheaval, perhaps pain, was exacerbated.

As granddaughter and grandmother resumed signing, Julia explained that Robert had to get a B on the quarter examination to have any chance to pass Algebra II, and he was sadly way behind. Julia explained that their thirty-minute lunch sessions would not be enough to get his math skills to a level where he could pass the next test and quizzes.

After explaining that Robert had sports practices every day after school and decided not to go back after school for extra help with Mr. Crampitz or meet with her, Grandmother Denise came up with an idea.

Denise suggested, "Tutor him here at night or on the weekend."

Julia was aghast. "You want me to ask a boy to come here to be alone with me?"

The quick-witted grandmother cajoled, "Julia, c'mon ... you aren't asking Robert to move in with you. Your mom and dad will be here, and if they can't, I'll chaperone this math clambake."

The idea was unnerving to Julia. It forced her to think of her deeper feelings about Robert. She resisted the urge to imagine the in-home tutoring with Robert, but as her grandmother warned, her heart's switch was "on," and she dared to think of herself working with Robert in the sitting room. The thought of it thrilled her but made her nervous in a way she had never known before.

Looking at her grandmother, Julia signed that the idea was preposterous as Mom and Dad would never allow it, Robert would never go for it, and this whole idea was making her nauseous.

Julia was a magnificently beautiful girl with long straight muted red hair, large oval hazel eyes, and an hourglass figure of 5 feet-5 inches, 116 pounds. With all that made her so pretty and very attractive, she had never been approached by a boy for a date. Not that she cared, nor did that cause her parents any concern. They realized that Julia's inability to talk probably deterred any interested young man from asking to spend time with her.

Backed by her grandmother's endorsement of the idea, Julia asked her parents for permission to host Robert Ragsdale for tutoring sessions in their home. When asked by her daughter, Emma, Julia's mother, proceeded to ask from the typical battery of questions parents ask about a boy, including, "Do we know his parents, and is he a gentleman?"

Then there was the inevitable question from the mother's perspective, "What does this Robert look like?"

Preparing to answer that last query, in her best descriptive signing, Julia responded, "Mom, Robert is tall. He has dark thick hair and brown eyes. He has incredible hands."

Instantly, all the warning lights went off in Emma's head, commenting, "What do you mean he has incredible hands? Where have his hands been that you think they are incredible?"

With the intervention and support of her grandmother, further questioning was derailed, and Julia set about the task of asking Robert if he wished to be tutored at her home.

Chapter 16

You Can Come to My Home

The more Julia thought about this idea of tutoring Robert at her home, the more awkward the whole idea became. Even though her parents had given their approval, there was much to be considered. Yes, Robert needed all the help he could get, or he probably wouldn't pass Algebra II. Yes, he wasn't going to get even a little break from Mr. Crampitz, no matter how hard he worked or scored on the examination.

Then there were some other obvious aspects of this plan that caused her some concern. Hold on a second. Carol Saphora was Robert's girlfriend, a steady thing indeed. How would she respond to his coming to Julia's house at night or on weekends? The most significant trepidation for Julia was how she was supposed to act around Robert. Working with him in the cafeteria, they were surrounded by other students. When the lunch wave was over, Robert would leave and go to his next class. Now here in the house, with no rigid time limits or people around, it would just be Robert and Julia sitting together. It was all getting scary.

That evening Julia took out a piece of her mother's parchment stationery and wrote a letter to Robert. In it, she outlined her offer to tutor him in Algebra II at her home on Main Street.

Tucking the brief letter in a matching envelope, she wrote his name, Robert Ragsdale, on the front and placed it in her bag to prepare for school the following day.

Julia's Monday morning walk down Main Street to school was filled with anticipation. She planned to give Robert the letter the first time she saw him, probably just before math class. To be sure, she was a little scared. What if Robert read the letter and didn't want to be tutored by her any longer? What if he shared the letter with others, especially Carol, and they all laughed at her?

Julia was still planning to help Robert with his Algebra II for one more week during lunch wave, but with the weekend behind him, he might have had a change of heart and decided not to be tutored any longer.

Never one to linger after Latin class, Julia scurried to math class this Monday, anxious to give Robert the letter. A hand grabbed her arm from the crowd of moving students, bidding her to stop. It was Robert. He smiled at her and asked, "Are we still on for lunch this week?"

Julia returned the grin and nodded in the affirmative. Then plummeting her hand into her book bag, she grabbed the letter and handed it to Robert.

Quizzically looking at Julia, he asked, "For me? Should I read it now?"

She nodded, and Robert immediately ripped open the letter. Reading it, his expression changed to one of fascination. Robert was touched by this overture of thoughtfulness and wondered, *Why would she do this for me?*

He hardly knew her, and few students even knew her by name, except that she was the kid who could hear but not speak.

Robert looked at the glowing face of Julia and stated, "Let me think about this."

Standing in the crowded hallway, Julia pulled out her pad and wrote, "Don't think too long. You have to pass the quarter exam."

Robert responded, "I know. I don't know what to do."

Now, in the crowded hallway, a voice interrupted, "I know what you can do. Cut out the gab with her and walk me to class." It was Carol, and she wasn't too happy.

Algebra II class was uneventful, but the previous week's quiz papers were handed back, and Robert did indeed pass it. Julia earned a perfect score, for which Mr. Crampitz remarked, "Well, Ms. Derigg (Julia) looks like you better continue to help Ragsdale. Maybe your brains are rubbing off on him."

After class, Robert said to Julia only, "I'll see you during lunch."

Sitting down at the corner table where she would tutor Robert, she saw Carol and him entering the cafeteria. Carol was waving her index finger in Robert's face, laying into him with some degree of anger. Julia felt terrible that she was probably the cause of that on-sided argument.

Robert sat down, and Julia immediately asked to see the quiz paper he had passed. Looking at his quiz paper, she started to show Robert the mistakes he had made. Robert placed his right hand on her left hand, halting her efforts, stating, "Let's talk."

Robert began, "Julia, it is so nice of you to want to help me with my Algebra II at your home. I would love to come to your home, and you can beat my brains in with algebra."

Joyful but worried, Julia observed, "What about Carol? I don't want to be the cause of any problem. Is she going to be ticked-off about all this?"

Robert declared, "Listen, I just cannot fail Algebra II. I can't, or I'm going to have to repeat the course. I told that to Carol, but she is kinda jealous and thinks I can get someone else, like a guy to tutor me."

"Why don't you?" suggested Julia.

Robert loudly railed back, "Because I want *you*."

Over at the table with Arthur Lefkowitz and the boys, Lefky overhead and shouted, "AND WE WANT YOU TOO."

Now Julia, just as embarrassed as Robert must have been, wrote on her pad, "Maybe, we better forget the entire idea."

Robert waited a few moments and spoke quietly to her, "Julia, can we start Wednesday night, say at 6:30 p.m.?"

For the first time, Julia stared into Robert's face, looking at him in a way that somehow frightened her.

She wrote on her pad, "Wednesday, 6:30 p.m."

Robert responded, "There is one problem. Where do you live?"

Julia wrote down her address. "535 Main Street."

Robert acting surprised and a little dumb. "You live on Main Street? So do I. I never knew that. I never saw you walking on Main."

With a sardonic look on her face, Julia wrote on her pad, "You never looked."

With Robert giggling and Julia pursing her lips in a smile, a twinkle in her eyes, the stage was set for Wednesday.

Chapter 17

Moments Become Memories

On Tuesday evening, with GaaGoo sleeping on her bed, Julia found it challenging to sleep and impossible to think of anything other than Robert. Denise, Julia's devoted grandmother, had decided to make an unscheduled trip across town to see her granddaughter on the eve of what might prove to be an interesting day.

Denise, an incomparable romantic who has a fascinating loving heart and had an incredible courtship with Julia's grandfather, Kyle, was caught up in this scenario of Julia's first, sort of, date with this boy, named Robert.

When Denise arrived at their North Main Street home, Emma, Denise's daughter and Julia's mother, told Denise that Julia was in her bedroom, already in bed. Denise slowly walked up the long staircase, thinking about the expectations of a young girl on the eve of a first date with a young man. She paused for a moment and remembered a day never to be forgotten in her life, when she and Kyle met after over ten years of searching for each other. Now she recalled the nervousness of that night. Many years later, here was her pretty granddaughter on the precipice of her first meeting with a young man.

Denise entered Julia's room, smiled warmly at her, and sat on the edge of her bed. Julia grabbed her grandmother in a loving embrace and then, pushing her back so she could communicate, signed, "Grandma, I'm sorry, I'm sorry, I do really like him."

Trying hard not to laugh, Denise responded, "I know, child, believe me, I know."

Julia signed, "What do I do, Grandma?"

Having always been blessed with compassion and wisdom, Denise said, "Julia, there are many life lessons, one of them is that we never know when a blessing is right around a corner. Initially, your teacher asked you to give this boy a helping hand. According to you, it led to daily tutoring that has already born fruit. Julia, you are an exceptional student, and by helping this student, you are helping yourself, discovering so much of what is deep inside of you. These are your God-given gifts. You are climbing forever up and growing as a woman. The best way to look at it is that you are 'lifting *Robert* while climbing.'"

Denise continued, "Julia, don't get ahead of yourself. You are about to lift Robert to a level where he might be able to pass Algebra II. Do him that service. If you have feelings for him, that's wonderful and something to experience for the first time in your life, but the task is to help him, and he does need your help. That's your purpose. Stay true to it."

Denise looked at her granddaughter and stood up to leave. Julia grabbed her left hand and pulled her back to the side of the bed, imploring an answer to her heart's burning question. She signed, "Grandmother, please tell me, how do you know if you love someone?"

In a moment of retrospection, Denise harkened back to a much earlier time in her life. Vividly, she remembered a day when she met a shy boy who was all too often the target of ridicule because he sought only to be left alone. Now, as a grandmother, she recalled the mistakes she made at Julia's age, specifically, how misdirected her teenage judgment had been, opting for a popular and attractive boy, only to discover the golden bliss of love with that almost-forgotten young man who searched for her for over a decade. Denise now drew the curtain back on that love in a flashing remembrance. For it was the love of the once-marginalized boy, Kyle, now her husband of many years, that brought forth the blessed lives of Emma, her daughter, Julia's mother, and Alexander, Denise and Kyle's son.

Filled with conflicted tears of fear for her granddaughter's vulnerable heart and the beauty that lies within a singular love, Denise spoke to Julia of love in the only words that came to her.

Denise slowly ran her fingers along Julia's long auburn hair, looking into her eyes. "Dear one, love is ever present in life because love is what you give, not what you get. It is easy to bask in the good feelings of received love, but what makes love the most perfect of life's gifts is to realize that love is less an emotion and more of an act of will. Beyond that, to answer your question, 'How will you know if you love someone?'"

Denise sighed and softly smiled. "Falling in love sometimes begins with the mere whisper of a word or a gentle rain falling on your face as you feel the presence of someone without a touch. You will know, you will know, my little one ... when you look upon a boy's face and see something that is 'beauty' to you. It will not be his nose, the dimple on his left cheek, or the tiny scar above his right eye, although you will note the minute location of each. Your heart will connect with your eyes and all your senses, and there will be the incandescent fragrance of something indefinable. Then in a whisper of an unspoken word from lips that make no sound, there will be a warmth as from a sustained summer breeze that will envelop you, maybe for all times.

"There is no singular answer to the doorway that is love. You will love in many ways. For some of those ways, it will mean giving of yourself when you know you truly give.

"You will know love by what you see and what you hear, not in the brashness of lightning bolts or firework, instead, the smile that appears on your face when no one is looking or by the fullness of your heart when you need to hear that special someone's voice."

Julia's eyes were illuminated in the need to understand that which is not understandable with words alone. She signed. "But, Grandmother, will his touch be different from anyone else? What will it feel like ... my hand in his? Will I be changed because he touched me?"

The insightful Denise slightly bowed, smiled, and considered that poets, artists, and philosophers have been trying to define the mysteries of love for centuries. All efforts to explain the manifestation of love will always fall short as "love" is for each heart to discover, feel, and share with another. Here she was talking with a teenager who was just beginning to be pierced sweetly in the heart by another.

It was time to end this discussion, say good night, and allow the cloak of first sleep to lead to a slumber of peaceful dreams. Denise kissed her granddaughter on the forehead and turned out the light on her nightstand, leaving with, "Julia, whatever tomorrow brings will be exactly as it is meant to be. Help Robert. Ask nothing more of the moment."

As Denise slowly descended the staircase, she was captivated by the innocent charm of the upcoming tutoring session. Before departing, her daughter Emma hugged her and stated matter-of-factly, "Mother, you will be here tomorrow."

Denise looked at her daughter and responded, "If you need me here."

Emma answered, "I think Julia needs you here. I know I just want my mother here as you have always been there for me."

"If you wish, but we need to give them their space. I'm sure there is someplace in this huge house we can hide out between 6:30 and 7:30 p.m."

As Julia dressed for school the following morning, her thoughts were beyond the new school day. There was no mention of anything related to the coming evening at breakfast with her parents. Scott, her father, talked with Emma, his wife, about his plans for the day and reminded her that he would be arriving home after 7:00 p.m. and not hold dinner for him as he would grab something to eat on the way home. Emma reminded her husband that Julia was expecting a guest this evening to help him with his math and that this student would probably be there when he got home.

As Julia picked up her bag in the foyer, opening the front door to walk to school, she looked back at her mother, who winked and asked, "Are you ready?"

Julia just smiled and headed out to Main Street for the fifteen-minute walk to the high school.

Chapter 18

This is Robert

At the conclusion of Algebra II class on Wednesday, Robert, seated in the back row, waited for Julia to exit the classroom and noted, "I'll see you tonight at your place."

Julia roughly tugged at his shirt sleeve, pulled out her pad, and wrote, "First, I will see you at lunch. Bring your book."

Robert got the message. Julia was not about to stop the lunch-wave tutoring because he was to receive extra help in math that evening. At their back table during lunch, neither Robert nor Julia made any mention of the 6:30 p.m. tutoring, except at the end of the lunch wave, when he departed with the words "Six thirty, I might be early" to her.

Rushing home after school, shortly before 3:00 p.m., Julia began to count the minutes until Robert's arrival. Despite the large confines and multiple rooms, she had never entertained anyone at home in her young life. All new to her this "entertaining," she tried to fill each anxious minute with activity. The sitting room, where they would work together, was spotless, as were all the rooms in the house, made that way by the two women who cleaned the house twice a week.

Julia laid out the materials she had prepared for Robert's instruction on the nineteenth-century French Renaissance table that they could sit at with two chairs brought over from the dining room down the hallway. So as not to scratch the ornate surface of the table, she covered it with a white lace tablecloth from the linen closet upstairs. Julia prepared her textbook for the tutoring session by placing paperclips on certain pages for quick reference.

Everything was ready by 5:00 p.m. Julia's mother reminded her that there was to be no food or drink in the sitting room. If she wanted to offer Robert water or a soft drink, she was to do so in the breakfast nook or the kitchen.

As the minutes ticked by, Julia went to her room to change out of the clothes she wore to school that day into an aqua-blue go-all-around, knife-sharp-pleated skirt with a white V-neck blouse with a ruffle collar and cuffs.

At 5:30 p.m., her grandmother arrived. Julia was reasonably anxious and immediately asked her grandmother to come upstairs to her bedroom. Although Julia was always neat and well-dressed, primarily because of her mother's guidance, she was never a clothing maven concerned about the latest fashions, but on this occasion, she wanted her grandmother's endorsement. Denise, who never minced words, was a tad taken aback by this sudden wave of vanity.

As soon as Grandmother Denise entered her room, Julia signed, "Grandma, do I look stupid?"

Denise scrunched up her face in response to the absurdity of the question. "No, Julia, you look absolutely adorable."

"ADORABLE?" Julia signed. "I don't want to look adorable. I want to look *good*."

Denise let out a hearty laugh and explained, "Honey, you look so good that swarms of bees will cover you with honey."

With that glib comment that only Denise could make, Julia handed her grandmother her comb, and Denise knew exactly what to do. As she had since Julia was hardly a year old, Denise combed out Julia's long straight auburn hair. Trying to take her mind off Robert, Denise spoke softly, "You know, you have your grandfather's hair color. Your mother or uncle didn't get his hair color, but you did. One of the first things I noticed about your Granddad was his hair, that was that red-gold color, auburn. It is so beautiful on you, especially with your hazel eyes. You are one beautiful girl, Julia."

Julia shook her head no. Denise continued, "You know, little one, Robert is coming here to solve math problems, helped by you, but he may have one big problem that he can't solve."

Standing in front of her mirror as her grandmother combed out her long hair, Julia signed, "What problem?"

Denise leaned into Julia's left ear. "Why *you*, of course. If he is not distracted by your hair, your eyes will paralyze him."

Julia smiled broadly and made a circular motion with her head, a gesture of happiness or humor that she had demonstrated throughout her life in the absence of speech. Her grandmother had succeeded in taking the edge off the moment at hand as Julia hugged her.

As the time drew near for Robert's entrance, the three generations of Denise, Emma, and Julia were seated at the breakfast nook, a built-in banquette in front of the bay window. It was the most casual place in a house brimming with formality. While Emma enjoyed an expresso, her mother, Denise, and her daughter, Julia, sipped on white tea (it must be Emperor's brand) from a Ginori Galli Rossi teapot. The chitchat was minimal as Julia watched the wall clock for the remaining minutes to tick away until Robert's arrival.

Shortly before 6:30 p.m., the door chimes rang. Julia jumped from her seat as her mother grabbed her arm. "Settle down, relax. It's just your guest. Take it easy."

As Julia got up from her seat at the breakfast nook to welcome her guest to the house, Denise suggested to Emma, "Let's give her some space. Let's just sit here until, or if, she calls us to join them so she can introduce us to the boy. I want to meet this young man as much as you do, but this is her moment. Let her have it."

Walking to the foyer, Julia hoped she looked "good." Once in the lobby, she opened the left door of the double front door that swung to the inside. There in the doorway was Robert. Nervously and instinctively, Julia signed, "Hello," forgetting that Robert did not know sign language.

Taken aback by the signing welcome, Robert said, "Julia, does that mean 'hello'?"

Julia nodded with a smile.

Robert, somewhat mesmerized by the grandeur of the foyer, scanned the row of paintings that were hung just above eye level and the marble floor at his feet. It occurred to him that this entranceway was bigger than his bedroom.

With his eyes darting about at the long twisting staircase, furnishings, and glass lamps, Julia took Robert by the arm and led him down the first-floor hallway of rooms, most of which were without doors by design. Each room appeared much more prominent and well lit because there were no doors.

Passing the study, an open room of ceiling-to-floor bookshelves, replete with elegantly framed paintings, memorabilia, and books, Robert suddenly stopped at the piano room. His eyes widened as he stood before the Steinway baby grand. Looking at Julia, he asked, "Do you play?"

With one nod of her head to gesture yes, Julia touched her hand to Robert's chest and then pointed to the black piano with the lid propped open. Looking puzzled, Robert asked Julia, "Are you asking me if I play the piano?"

In a million years, Julia could not have anticipated his answer.

Robert hesitated for a moment, and then with a deep breath and looking into Julia's face, the tall Robert replied, "Yes." Robert continued, "Are you surprised?"

Julia again nodded that she was taken aback but surmised that this basketball player's musical repertoire was probably nothing more than "Jingle Bells," "Happy Birthday to You," and the always elemental "Chopsticks."

Robert sensed Julia's disbelief. For reasons he could not immediately discern, Robert explained this little secret and began, "Julia, I have been playing piano since I was six years old. My parents insisted that I learn the piano. My mother plays."

Julia grabbed her pad and wrote, "My mother plays."

Robert continued, "I wanted no part of playing the piano, but I cooperated and took private lessons with my parents' agreement that they would tell not anyone and never make me play in front of friends and relatives. If you want to know why I'll tell you. I love playing sports, and I'm pretty good at basketball, but I saw how the guys made fun of other kids learning instruments or taking singing or dancing lessons, ugh. I never wanted the other guys to know. I didn't want anyone making fun of me. My parents have been good about keeping it quiet as long as I continue to practice every day. I played in a few recitals downstate and two out-of-state competitions but never around town."

Robert continued his confession, "I never said this to anyone before, but my piano teacher, Dr. Treonderdaris, told me that I was his best student and that I could be a great pianist someday. Hard to believe, huh? Mr. Stupid Algebra II student here who plays piano."

Julia's expression changed to a scowl and with her left hand, motioned three or four short waves in front of his mouth as if to say, "You are not stupid."

Julia was intrigued by Robert's puzzling revelation and wrote on her pad, "I'm not sure I believe you. You are popular in school. Why would anyone make fun of you?"

Robert took Julia's hand in his and responded, "Julia, how could anyone make fun of you, but you know they do, don't you?"

Tears came to Julia's eyes, hearing the confirming comment that some students have made fun of her because she cannot talk.

"I'm sorry. I'm so sorry. I shouldn't have said what I did," uttered Robert. "Do you want me to leave now?"

Julia glared at the tall Robert and waved her right index finger in front of his face. Taking pen to her pad once again, she wrote, "I will never make fun of you, ever. Shouldn't we get to the math?"

Feeling so horrible for making Julia cry, Robert almost began to cry himself.

Julia wrote on her pad once again. "Will you do something for me?"

Robert read it and with regret, nodded yes.

Seeking to mend his heart and damaged confidence, Julia wrote on her pad, "Please play something for me now."

"No, I couldn't. I've taken too much of your time already, and we have math to do."

Julia stepped to the black leather piano bench and pointed at it that he should sit down *now.*

Realizing that this sensitive, caring girl had just cornered him, Robert asked, "Play what for you?"

Julia wrote once again and underlined on the pad, "Your best!"

Smiling and assuming they were alone in this enormous house, Robert told her, "Well, I will not play 'Chopsticks.'"

Filled with a need to laugh and couldn't, she made a circular motion with her head as Robert wondered if she was all right, making this head movement. In less than fifteen minutes, Robert had made her cry and want to laugh.

Once again, she emphatically pointed at the piano bench, demanding Robert sit and play. Seating himself on the black leather piano bench, he adjusted its height. Awed at the majesty of this Steinway baby grand piano, he lifted the fallboard covering the keys and found himself in position to play the finest piano he had ever seen or touched.

Julia positioned herself near the front of the piano, along the top board long prop so she could look at Robert. If this turned out to be a bad idea, maybe embarrassing to him, she wanted to be close enough to smile and assure him that everything would be OK.

Robert looked up through the open piano lid at Julia. He did not smile, but his eyes stared into Julia's as if something dire was about to happen.

Robert looked down at the keyboard where his long thin fingers were positioned to play. Whatever Robert had chosen to play, it was a piece he had committed to memory. It began with a dramatic cord. That single cord, followed by the most gentle touch on the keyboard, tweaked the ears of Julia's mother and grandmother, who were still seated at the breakfast nook at the far end of the first floor.

Emma, Julia's mother, a talented ballet dancer who studied classical piano in her youth, immediately identified the music. "Mother!" Emma exclaimed to her mother, Denise. "Do you know what that is?"

Not waiting for an answer from her perpetually beautiful mother, she continued, "Oh my lord, that is the first movement of Beethoven's 'Pathétique Sonata,' No. 8 in C Minor. That's our piano, but who is playing? Julia doesn't have that ability."

Denise and Emma immediately left their tea and coffee to investigate. The music grew louder as they walked down the hallway to the piano room. There in the piano room with Julia standing, looking mesmerized; a young man was playing the Steinway. Dramatically, this dark-haired boy was elegantly flattering the keyboard with delicate dexterity. Entering the piano room, mother and grandmother assumed a place on either side of Julia, captured by the incredible talent being unveiled before them. Emma spoke softly to her daughter, "And just who is this pianist, *the immortal* Glenn Gould, no less?"

Julia's eyes, never leaving Robert, signed, "No, Mother ... This is Robert."

Robert's eyes were transfixed on the ivory keys as his straight thick black hair flopped about his forehead. Julia's fingers were slowly moving as if touching Robert's fingers as her eyes shared the emotion of his eyes as he brought forth a sound she had never heard from that piano.

Emma absorbed every note, recalling her piano instructor's explanation of the sonata form of this piece. She listened intently and remembered her teacher's words, *"The Pathétique is believed to have been selected by Beethoven himself to convey a romantic and even sorrowful mood of the sonata."*

Denise's heart soared as she watched her glowing granddaughter's face. With Emma spellbound in the flowing music, Denise was lost in the wonderment of watching her granddaughter, who was speaking without words through her dazzling hazel eyes, absorbing everything that was Robert. As for Julia, she was adrift on a sea of sight and sound as the beat of her heart sang a perfect harmony to all that was Robert. Denise felt Julia's passion as she first felt the intensity of love when her husband Kyle brought her spirit to life, discovering supreme love so many years ago.

Robert's hands made the first movement of Beethoven's piece come alive with a dark and dramatic introduction before assuming the traditional sonata's brisk, nearly frenetic motion.

His talent and skill on the keyboard were unmistakable, but Julia fell to the depths of love with certainty amid his notes, lines, and spaces.

For ten minutes, Robert played without a word or interruption. There was no requisite effort to applaud at the music's end as too much emotion had filled the piano room. With Robert's last note, he looked up from the keyboard to see Julia with a quivering lower lip and her eyes embracing his.

Robert stood and asked, "Julia? Was my 'best' OK enough?"

Holding back tears of never-before realized emotions, Julia crossed her arms over her chest in a "hug" gesture.

Standing tall at six-foot-one-inch, Robert towered over Julia, her mother, and her grandmother. As if any introduction was necessary at this moment, he politely introduced himself, "Mrs. Derigg," not knowing which of the two adult women was Julia's mother, "my name is Robert Ragsdale."

Emma extended her hand to shake his and responded, "Robert, it is a pleasure to know such a talented young man. This is my mother, Julia's grandmother, Denise."

Although this was Julia's moment, Emma had to take the time to inquire, "Robert, where did you learn to play? Your technique and interpretation of the sonata were impeccable."

Robert humbly accepted the compliment. "Mrs. Derigg, I've been under the teaching of the maestro, Dr. Vasileios Treonderdaris."

Julia's mother continued, "Someone with your talent should be known to the world, young man."

Getting defensive, Robert said, "Mrs. Derigg, I'm a basketball player. I think I'm a pretty good one. I just happen to play the piano, and I try to keep that as quiet as possible. I played in front of you just now because Julia, more or less, insisted that I do, but I would not want it getting out that I play the piano."

Always inquisitive and pragmatic, Denise pointedly solicited, "And what do you want to do, Robert Ragsdale?"

"I want to pass Algebra II," confessed Robert.

"And then what, may I ask?" Denise examined further.

Robert, who had not been subjected to this type of rapid-fire questioning from relative strangers before, responded, "I wish to go to college and hopefully play basketball there. That's as far as my plans go at this point."

Denise, sensing that this back-and-forth was becoming uncomfortable for Robert, "Well then, maybe we better let you and Julia 'begin the beguine' (a reference to a song that she long ago danced to with her husband Kyle) and start your mathematical work."

Emma laughed, commenting, "Oh, Mother, you and your romantic songs. Is there anything you and Dad ever did that was not romantic?"

Winking at her daughter, Emma, Denise retorted, "Never."

With that cheeky question-and-answer, Denise directed, "Emma, let us adjourn to the breakfast nook for a refreshed cup of tea and one of your expressos that is strong enough to take barnacles off the USS *Constitution*. These two need to get to their math work."

Denise and Emma returned to the breakfast nook without much talk between them. Sitting at the table, as the tea was brewing and expresso percolating, Denise began to cry. Emma immediately noticed, "Mother, are you all right?"

Denise looked at her daughter with loving eyes. "Em, I haven't felt quite like this since you danced Clara in *The Nutcracker*."

Emma fondly remembered her evening as the lead dancer in *The Nutcracker* ballet. "Mom, what made you think of that night?"

Denise recalled and connected the moments of the last few minutes. "Did you see your daughter as she listened to Robert play? Did you feel the stirring in her heart and how captivated she was? That was how your father and I felt, watching you enthrall the audience at the Opera House. I never thought I would see or feel anything like that again."

Listening to her mother's words, Emma suggested, "Mother, I think there is more to what just happened at the Steinway than Beethoven."

The intuitive Denise remarked, "Emma, your daughter is in the middle of a 'Robert tidal wave,' and she is just beginning to understand what 'overwhelming' means ... as in she's in love up to her pretty eyes."

Shall We Algebra?

Escorting Robert from the piano room, Julia led Robert to the sitting room, only that it had no doors and stood open to the hallway. There they sat at the long French Renaissance table. Julia opened her math book with page markers already in place. She began with a factoring review, writing math examples to illustrate each principle. Looking up from her pad and text to see if Robert understood all she was trying to show him, she found Robert looking directly at her. Julia wrote on the pad, "Are you getting this, or am I going too fast?"

Robert let out a sniffing chuckle.

Julia wrote furiously on her pad, "Are you too tired to work on math?"

Robert smiled with an emphatic, "No!"

"Robert," she wrote, "then what's your problem? You aren't paying attention. This is important stuff if you want to understand how to solve Algebra II problems."

Bowing slightly and looking up through his eyebrows, "Julia, I really like you."

Pursing her lips with a serious stare, Julia shook her head left to right a few times, indicating an adverse reaction or just a "nooo."

Julia pointed down with her left index finger at the open math text, glaring at Robert.

Robert grabbed her index finger, holding it tightly as Julia looked at her finger wrapped in his hand, growing uneasy.

Robert repeated but separated his words, "Julia ... I ... like ... you."

With that reiterated sentence, Robert brought Julia's held index finger to his lips and gently kissed the tip of her finger.

Julia instantly pulled her finger away, blinking her eyes as a tear flowed down her right cheek.

Embarrassed, Robert said, "I'm sorry, Julia. I'm a jerk. I had no business doing that. Maybe I should leave."

Julia's heart pounded, and she was having difficulty catching her breath. Julia felt there was something she was supposed to do in this instance, but all she could do was look at Robert's face, a mere foot and a half from hers. Again shaking her head, she got up from her seat and walked down the hallway, trying to escape this strange feeling and situation.

At the end of the hallway, she saw her mother and grandmother talking over tea. Julia's mother's back was to her as Julia entered, but Grandmother Denise immediately saw the flushed cheeks and tear track on Julia's right cheek.

Denise signed. "OK, easy now ... What happened?"

Julia responded in sign, "Grandmother, he said he liked me ... twice. Then he kissed my finger."

Denise felt that Julia's innocence would come tumbling down soon enough to Robert, but a "finger kiss"?

Denise got up from her chair and hugged her granddaughter and whispered to her, "You're OK. Everything is going to be OK. Relax, just relax. So he likes you, does he?"

Julia moved back from the hug with wide-open eyes and gave a rapid nodding. In her well-known pragmatic nature, Denise suggested, "So go back in there and teach the boy some math."

Julia, somewhat surprised to hear this suggestion, shook her head no.

With a grandmother's love in her voice, Denise directed, "Now get back in there and give him what he came here for."

Julia nodded, left the breakfast nook as Denise smiled and reconsidered the words she had just spoken to Julia. *Now I wonder what Robert did come here for?*

Taking her seat beside Robert, Julia began to illustrate the components of factoring once again. Still somewhat embarrassed from the kissing of her index finger, Robert assumed a more focused demeanor and followed her instruction.

Minutes led to an hour, and with his impromptu piano recital, Robert realized he would be late picking up his girlfriend Carol and meeting their friends at the Wilkinson Theater for a movie. Julia was strident and continued writing on her pad. Sometimes, just as she had done in the cafeteria tutoring sessions, she placed her hand on his to help him slowly solve the example she wrote out before him.

In the middle of solving a problem, Robert chanced to look at his watch. It was 8:30 p.m. and dreadfully late. He thought to ask Julia if he could use her phone to call Carol and make up some reason for his tardiness but thought it best just to leave and drive over to Carol's house.

Rather abruptly, Robert rose from his chair and looked down at this face that he now found to be captivating. "Julia, I have to go. I'm late, and I just have to go."

Julia got up from her chair, and with chills raking through her, she pointed up to Robert's lips with her index and middle finger of her left hand, almost in a stabbing motion. Robert did not move or know what Julia was trying to convey to him, looking up into his eyes, slightly parting her lips, so wanting to talk, so needing to say words. Instead, she took Robert's left hand with both of her hands.

Julia clutched Robert's index finger with her left hand and held it in front of him with her eyes drinking in his brown eyes. Raising his seized finger to her face, Julia kissed his left index finger and then moving it away from her for a second, kissed his finger again.

There was nothing more to communicate between them today.

Robert, unable to find the words to express his feelings in the curtain of emotions that draped them, stated, "Thank you, Julia. Thank you. I have to go. Talk soon".

Julia smiled at Robert's casual, unthinking last two words, indeed said to anyone else, and taking pad and pencil in hand, she wrote, "I WISH."

Again, Robert was left embarrassed, but Julia took him by the arm and led him off to the front door.

With no time left and thoughts running chaotically through them, Robert departed as Julia stood in the open left side of the front door. Robert trotted quickly down the cobblestone walkway to where his car was parked. Julia wanted to smile as his car pulled away, but she cried. She felt empty inside, but she was full—full of this boy Robert who plays basketball, plays the piano better, and needs to learn his multiplication table.

As Julia dined with her parents, completed homework, and practiced her piano, her thoughts were of Robert Ragsdale all through the evening. She wished she could share her thoughts with someone, and more than ever, she wanted to speak about her feelings. Julia needed to express her thoughts as everything about this boy Robert felt weird. Something was very different inside of her, and she wished her mother or grandmother were there to understand her feelings without saying words.

Chapter 19

A Class Election

Since entering the high school, each class is indoctrinated into the small and large steps that will provide added incentive for academic achievement and its impact on post-high school opportunities. One of the rituals at the beginning of the new school term is the election of junior class officers. More of a tradition than a common-sense decision, the election occurs as students inaugurate the final two years of their secondary education, a critical period in each student's life, making choices that will impact the rest of their days. There is a seriousness of purpose during this time as each classroom grade and activity affects the direction one will take in life after the high school years are complete. Students in their junior and senior years, known as upper-class men and women, become aware of every choice and decision they make.

As with many schools across the country, understanding the importance of the democratic process as an experiential function, students are subsequently elected as "class officers" with nothing more than a two-minute speech before classmates and a few handcrafted posters. Most students and some thoughtful educators recognize the process for what it is, "a popularity contest."

Since the junior high school years, grades seven through nine, the same group of students has been elected year after year, and a few ran unopposed, further validating the premise that most students viewed class officer elections as more an "ordination" than an election. This circumstance minimized a meaningful engagement of most students as the election of four class officers felt more like a foregone conclusion.

Once passing through the sophomore year in the high school, students generally acknowledged the added stature of becoming an upper-class person. The election of class officers for the junior year held added significance for members of each junior class, a very different feeling from the almost rubber-stamp elections of previous years in school when only popular persons need apply.

As per school tradition, the junior class officers, elected in early fall, last week in September, were the students who directly collaborated with town leaders to create the largest annual event in town, the annual First Lighting of the Lantern Gala, always the most exciting and colorful event of the school year. While the junior and senior promenades had their own grandeur, each served only individual classes with limited funds for the staples of those traditional events, including music, decorations, and some refreshments.

With the typical implied responsibilities of class or school organizational officers, such as the secretary recording meeting minutes and the president chairing the occasional meetings that are called, the junior class officers are required to attend each meeting of the First Lighting of the Lantern committee. They must fully participate in every task, from the action plan for the event to the design of the dance card.

Make no mistake, whoever was elected, the junior class officers must be work-driven student leaders. Since the opening of the high school in 1916, there have always been many more important tasks and responsibilities that require overt student leadership of the junior class officers than the sophomore or senior officers. As the Lantern gala was the most significant event of the town each year, the junior class offices were held accountable for bringing this event to life.

Since the initial design of Wallingford's first comprehensive secondary school, the high school, the town's people, led by the House of Burgesses, the community's board of elected officials, felt that the high school, especially given that it was the largest community-funded structure in town history, must be a center of more than just secondary education. The structural design included a state-of-the-art school with a balconied auditorium at the center of the building with hand-painted seating. However, the town's leadership insisted that the student framework of their secondary school include the integration and active participation in the Wallingford community. Town leader Arnold T. Hubbard stated, "We must train our young people to be responsible future leaders, and to accomplish that, we must engage and empower them to participate in community activities."

By traditional plan and expectation, the four junior officers will be required to lead the annual Legend of the First Lighting of the Lantern Gala each November. The lavishly decorated extravaganza event captures the community's attention, always held on the high school's courtyard, facing Main Street. Generations of men and women don their finery to cavort on the courtyard once again, refreshing the tender memories of times gone by.

With all the recognition and challenging work inherent in this event for the junior officers, the adult members of the community's collaboration committee for the gala shower privilege and the figurative spotlight on the elected officers. The formal attire of the junior officers is created for each officer without monetary charge to them. Each officer is driven to the gala in a horse-drawn carriage with the name of the junior officer prominently displayed on each carriage.

Most dramatically, each of the four officers, with their chosen escort, leads the always majestic opening procession and heads the receiving line.

The recognition afforded the junior class officers is extreme indeed. However, some students believe these *annually recycled popular* officers do not represent the best of their class.

At the forefront of that point of view and an outspoken proponent that "something must be done" was Arthur Lefkowitz, everyone's Lefky.

Heretofore, when Lefky gets his proverbial teeth in an issue, he will usually do something in reaction, but whatever his ploy, it will usually be diabolical and unexpected.

Chapter 20

Cafeteria Chicanery and Confrontation

Since school cafeterias came into being in the twentieth century, they have been far more than just a place to draw down on a hot lunch or eat from a brown bag. The "lunch wave," a predetermined group of students, is a period in the school day when students sit where they want, with whom they choose, socialize, and *usually* eat something.

Generally speaking, students sit at tables of six with those who offer a degree of social collegiality, considered to be friends, with a banter of common interests, a dose of gossip, sarcasm, critical comments directed at anyone in shouting distance, and large amounts of jocularity. It is a period all students anticipate, away from the classrooms and adult-driven instruction, where plans are made for after-school hours. The lunch wave is also a time when flirting skills are honed through observation and trial and error.

During the lunch wave, there is the potential for contentious moments when students will openly find fault with one another, precipitating confrontation, such as the traditional food fight. Illustrated in throwing a single meatball at a student to flinging everything food at a neighboring table, supervising teachers and administrators are always on guard for the signs of a student-to-student confrontation.

However, there is one more product of the *social incubator* known as the school cafeteria; it spawns youthful plots and schemes.

On this September day, the buzz around the cafeteria was the start of the impending annual process of electing the all-important junior class officers who would play a significant role in the annual First Lighting of the Lantern Gala.

Although the members of the Faculty Leadership Council, the volunteer leadership group of the teachers, had yet to announce the deadline for the submission of applications for office-holding of the junior class, a few perennial holders of class office were already spreading their popular smiles to members of the class.

Circulating around the second lunch wave tables were two students who had been sophomore class officers in the previous year, both parenthetically had run as unopposed candidates dating back to their junior high school years. Cathy Reynolds, a cheerleader, was the long-standing class secretary, but no one in the class wanted any part of the secretary position, maybe because they might have to do something like preparing meeting minutes. Heretofore, cute and ditzy Cathy had scooted through the years as the assumed office-holder.

The perennial president of the class going back to the sixth grade was the energetic Bonnie Bentz, whose distinctive walk was often imitated by fellow students. Appearing to walk on her toes, Bouncing Bonnie, as she was often called, would swing her arms outwardly as if her elbows were wired to her ribcage. Bonnie is a consistent achiever in all her classes and is involved in many school organizations, from the marching band to the pep club. She is acknowledged by fellow students and teachers alike as the epidemy of a "brownnoser," whose lack of sincerity is only exceeded by her bluster and bravado. The totality of the Bonnie Bentz persona has made her one of the, if not *the*, most popular students in the school and an unopposed candidate for class president. No one would dare to run against the pretentious Bouncing Bonnie.

On this fateful September Friday, Bonnie and her sidekick, Cathy Reynolds, made the rounds of the cafeteria tables and approached the table headed by Arthur Lefkowitz and his cronies. As ever, Lefky held court during his lunch wave with some of his buddies, known as his tribe, Gerald Banderino, Arsenella Holcomb, and George Owelowski. Bouncing Bonnie audaciously reminded all those at the table to make sure they vote when the election of junior class officers takes place. Lefky, seizing on this opportunity to stir the pot, asked Bonnie, "So who's running for president this year? Anyone we know?"

Bonnie shot back, "Well, *I am,* of course," then added with a big toothy smile, "Who else do you need"?

A bit of a hush came over the table and surrounding tables that recognized a Bouncing Bonnie versus Lefky confrontation. Lefky continued, "Maybe someone will run against you who will actually do something for our class."

Bonnie reared up in self-righteousness, "And who wants to run against me for president? You, Arthur? What have you ever done? Don't make me laugh. You couldn't win an election for class jerkweed if no one else were running."

The proverbial gauntlet was cast down before Lefky with a glare. It was one thing to cast aspersions about Lefky behind his back, but to stick it in his face in front of others was tantamount to a declaration of war, and Lefky was now all-in and would bring to bear the fullness of his diabolical creativity.

It was no secret that Lefky detested teacher favoritism. Whether at a table during the lunch wave or at a booth at the Sweet Shop, Lefky was never quiet, often speaking out about inequities as he saw them.

Lefky was always pontificating on how some teachers "treated some of us guys who didn't take their highfalutin classes (such as Algebra II, Latin III, and English Literature)." Lefky was forever beating the drum that "us guys who take printing, machine trades, and small engine repair will someday be the men with the money in town."

At the top of Lefkowitz's perpetual complaint list was how the same dozen or so students kept getting all the attention, winning all the school awards, gaining privileges, and the most irritating of all for Lefky, was the election of these same students to class officers.

It was not just that these were the students who most of the teachers thought were "something special." It was that they usually ran unopposed. Nobody wanted to waste their time running against them. To make matters worse, some students who might have considered a run for class office were dissuaded from running because to get on the ballot, a student had to have a completed nomination form with the signatures of three current members of the Faculty Leadership Council.

Chapter 21

Constructing The Plot

The pranks and schemes of the past all had their day, but few were of a more personal nature for Lefky than renovating the election of junior class officers. Following the rather pointed altercation with Bonnie Bentz in the cafeteria on the sensitive issue of class officer elections, Lefky asked his tribe to meet him when the Sweet Shop opened on Saturday at 11:00 a.m. for a "powwow."

As it was early, owner Joe Connors asked to sit with the boys. At their regular booth at the back of the Sweet Shop were Bando, Arse, Owl, and Lefky. Lefky, not holding back, immediately expressed his displeasure with the insult leveled at him by Bouncing Bonnie, but he was adamant that even without the insult, the junior class elections this year could not be allowed to continue as "business as usual."

Sweet Shop owner Joe Connors, fully aware of Lefky's rather no-holds-barred reputation for chicanery, was instantly drawn into a Lefky plot unfolding and called out, *"I'm in!* What can I do?"

All the boys laughed at the very idea of an adult knitting in with them, but what the tribe didn't know was how much a part of the Lefky plot Joe would be willing to play.

Even though the personal affront leveled by Bonnie Bentz in the cafeteria was not even twenty-four hours ago, Lefky's scheming wheels were turning with aerodynamic downforce.

Lefky spoke his ideas for the changing of circumstances of the junior class elections. He stated that some candidates for class office, and there hadn't been more than five for years, were probably righteous people. What he thought they, the tribe and he, ought to do is focus on getting, "a candidate of their choice elected as class president," and as he put it, "dethroning Bouncing Bonnie."

Bando wasted no time bringing up the obvious. "So who and where do we find a junior willing to be a candidate for president? After all, Bonnie had run unopposed since we were back in sixth grade."

Lefky proposed, "We need a candidate we can sell to all the junior class members, someone who has appeal, someone who will surprise everyone so that every class member will want to stand up and vote for that person. This has got to be a student who might seem like a joke because we are supporting him or her, but it will be no joke when we give the class the hottest campaign they have ever seen."

In his raucous manner with an ample dose of profanity, Arse suggested, "We need to do more than surprise the class members. We have to freakin' shock them, and by the time all the ballots are cast, we will have won the election. After all, I don't think many people like Bonnie anyway. The teachers love her ass because she is the ultimate brownnoser, but beyond holding all these offices, she has done nothing for the junior class. She has always run unopposed. There has been no one with the guts to go against her. Here is the real issue. There hasn't been a choice. Over the years, no one in our class has been given a real alternative for class president. It has been Bonnie Bentz, year after year. We need to give the class a choice."

Lefky barked, "We have to bushwack this election, do something no one expects. Bonnie cannot know what hit her. We must put someone up against her that she will figure has no chance against her, make her overconfident so that she will say something dumb in her speech or on her silly-ass posters and then make our candidate everybody's candidate."

Chapter 22

Whom Can We Get to Run?

Each member of the tribe at the table and Mr. Connors had ideas. Squinting up his face in concentration, Bando suggested, "Let's run one of the most beautiful girls in the school against ole teethy Bonnie. How about Joey Galacious? She's hotter than hell and a born kibitzer. She'll flirt with every boy in the school."

Lefky responded to the Joey idea, "Yeah, she'll talk the pants off anyone. Yeah, she is a campaigner for sure. She will piss off every female member of the class, flirting with the boyfriend of every girl." The election will be lost before it starts.

Owl interjected, "Why do we have to get a girl candidate? It's too bad Robert Ragsdale has already been a class officer. He'd be perfect to beat Bouncing Bonnie, but he wouldn't run against her for president. He's too much of a gentleman for that. Besides, Robert will probably run again for class vice president. He's an honorable dude."

Lefky spoke thoughtfully about his general plan and detailed some of the steps, "First, we have to find a person willing to run, who will do what we say during the campaign. Then we have to get that student nominated, which means, we have to get three members of the faculty council to sign off on the nomination form," another aspect of the class elections that Lefky thought was unfair.

Arse interrupted, "Did we forget? We have to find a candidate, *our* candidate, who can speak from that big-ass podium in the auditorium *and* has a speech that will get everyone's attention." Arse asserted, "*Nobody* wants to get in front of other students and talk. That would be like the worst oral report of all time. No one will do that even for us. We're screwed."

Lefky would not be deterred and demanded that everyone think harder.

Mr. Connors, sitting with the tribe during this discussion and noting the seriousness of their purpose, offered, "I say we don't make a decision on a dry palate. Cherry Cokes on me, and let's get a little music floating to help us think."

Mr. Connors asked his waitress, Sheila, to bring cherry Cokes for everyone seated in the booth except him. She brought him a black coffee as Joe fiddled with the back of the jukebox and played his favorite song, no. 16, "Green Onions" by Booker T. & the M.G.'s.

As they sipped their beverage, Bando declared, "We are making this too hard. Our problem isn't that complicated."

Between the sips of cherry Coke and the finger-drumming by Mr. Connors to the riffs of "Green Onions," Lefky raised his eyes to look at Owl. George "Owl" Owelowski was tall, always dressed with his shirt tail out, and walked slowly. Suddenly, it hit Lefky—with a little work, maybe a lot of hard work, he could make Owl look *presidential*. Another factor didn't escape Lefky's thought process: Owl would do just about anything Lefky wanted, and they needed a pliable candidate. After all, Owl pulled the fire alarm before the "basketball ticket scam." At Lefky's behest, it was Owl who filled the trash paper basket of Mr. Florastein, typing teacher, with water, and then he floated the fake puke after Lefky became aware Mr. Florastein was making a habit of hovering over the girls in his typing class, looking down their blouses. Yes, Owl made sense to Lefky, but would he do it?

Finally, Lefky looked directly at Owl and declared, "Owl, you are our next class president."

Arse, Bando, and Mr. Connors let out a collective cheer with applause upon hearing those words.

Sitting across Lefky, Owl was stunned and instantly shook his head *no*! However, Lefky was not easily denied or turned down. All the others seated in the booth smiled their approval. Owl kept shaking his head and saying no.

George Owelowski or Owl, a nickname hung on him by Lefky years ago, is an angular young man of 5 foot-10 inches, maybe 155 pounds; he was one of the quietest students in the school and a surefire nominee in a senior class superlative category, "Shyest Boy," when he became a senior. Owl was unassuming, intelligent, and a solid B student who rarely volunteered in class. He had soft blue eyes and dirty blond hair coiffured too long for his thin face. George found Lefky to be "a scream," admiring his bravado, and was proud to be considered one of Lefky's inner circle, one of the tribe.

Each person in the booth had an encouraging comment on why Owl should be their candidate for junior class president.

Mr. Connors said, "Owl, this can open up doors for you in the future. This could be a whole new *you*."

"You might get some really good-looking girls to talk to you," asserted Arse.

Always the quasi-enforcer for Lefky and the boys, Bando said, "Owl, you will run for president of our junior class, and you *will* win ... Or I will definitely kick your ass."

Finally, it was Lefky's turn to seal the deal of Owl on his candidacy for office. "Owl, I wouldn't have picked you if you couldn't win. Owl, I wouldn't ask you to do this if I didn't think you would make a great class president. You better get something through your head. This means a lot to the entire junior class, so don't be selfish. Oh, and one more thing you better never forget ... I ASKED YOU TO BE OUR CANDIDATE FOR CLASS PRESIDENT."

It was now inevitable to Owl that he was the selected candidate to dethrone Bouncing Bonnie Bentz. Almost on the verge of tears, the shy, reserved George Owelowski, a.k.a. Owl, lamented, "Lefky, guys," meaning the others at the powwow booth, "I have never made a speech in my life ... never shook a hand, except to say goodbye to my uncle Martin when he moved out of the house, and I've never even put my arm around a girl. How do you expect me to win?"

Mr. Connors, who always loved the young people he served in his Sweet Shop, with all their challenges and triumphs, let Lefky lay out a bit of the plan he and Lefky had surreptitiously discussed last evening before the Sweet Shop closed.

With attention to detail, Lefky began to roll out the plan.

Lefky said, "First, there are seven women teachers on the Faculty Leadership Council. On Monday afternoon, immediately after school, when half the student body is on the courtyard, I will meet Owl at the back door, near the parking lot, and give Owl five white roses. Then Owl will go to the classrooms of Ms. Peterson, Ms. Chloride, and Mrs. Bradersen and present each of them with a rose with the request, and you have to memorize this line, Owl, 'My name is George Owelowski. Would you honor my candidacy for junior class office by signing my nomination form'?"

Owl already felt nervous about the operation. "Lefky, I never had any of these teachers for any subject. They don't even know me."

"Don't be concerned, Owl. The rose will catch them off guard, and each will be flattered. They might ask you a question or two, so just be honest."

Owl inquired, "So what could they ask me?"

Lefky was prepared. "One of them might ask why you want to run for class president."

Owl, looking sheepishly, hesitated. "Well, why *do* I want to run for class president? Do I answer, ''Cause Lefky told me to?'"

Lefky responding harshly, "No, Owl ... this is what you answer, 'Ms. or Mrs. So-and-So, my only desire is to serve every member of the junior class to the best of my ability.'"

Bando asked the obvious question, "Hey, Lefky, who the hell is Ms. So-and-So?"

Mr. Connors let out a hearty laugh with an offhanded comment. "Maybe I should open another store and name it 'Brains Are Us.'" Mr. Connors explained to Bando, "'So-and-So' is just a general term for any of their last names.

Lefky was using 'So-and-So' as a general reference to teach Owl what to say when he talks to each of the teachers."

Now fully immersed in their collective efforts, Arse pointed at Owl. "Remember, this is an important point: Don't call any of those teachers Ms. So-and-So, or you'll look like an ass."

Chapter 23

A Theme Emerges

Although Owl was far from convinced that he could do all the stuff that the tribe expected of him, he was sure that everything Lefky said he, Owl, could do, Lefky would make happen. The completed nomination forms must have three signatures and all the other information by this Friday, September 19. The election would be at the end of the month. As Owl would request the signatures of three members of the Faculty Leadership Council on Monday (with flowers), if any of those teachers refused to sign, Lefky would tell Owl which teachers on the faculty council to approach next. Lefky was confident that the three teachers he selected to have Owl ask for their signatures would comply, so the campaign would have to be in full swing by the following Monday.

Over many years, it is apparent to one and all that class officer election posters were of little practical use. They were often put up by a candidate just because it was a "fun" activity, prepared with the help of parents, and put up by some well-meaning fellow students. School campaign posters have been a relative waste of time, *unless* the campaign posters for a candidate are designed to introduce a new candidate who had never held office and for a student who hardly had marginal name recognition within the class. The tribe and Mr. Connors realized this was a ground-up campaign; meaning, they had to create name recognition and a buzz around their candidate, Owl.

After an hour and multiple glasses of cherry Cokes, the tribe and Mr. Connors focused on the actual campaign for Owl. They started to ask one another questions about Owl. Arse asked Owl directly, "So what have you ever done?"

Owl looked at Arse and responded, "Nothing! Can I go home now?"

Mr. Connors said to the tribe and Sheila, the waitress, who just happened to be hovering over the candy counter, "The question is not what has Owl done but what does Owl do."

Sheila yelled out, "Owl hoots!"

The tribe and Mr. Connors hesitated to react for a second and then broke out into laughter. "That's right," responded Bando, "everyone knows that an owl hoots."

Immediately, Lefky latched on to the words. "We will build the campaign to have everyone in the junior class ... HOOOOOOT. When asked simple questions, like 'How was the football game?' we need to get every student to respond 'hoot.' If someone asks, 'Will I see you on the courtyard after school?' The answer is 'hoot.'"

Through a series of ideas, high-spirited laughs, and giggles, Bando offered, almost tongue in cheek, "We must get every class member to 'hoot for Owl.'"

A bell went off in Mr. Connors's head, advancing the word farther. He declared, "The word hoot must be shouted/yelled to symbolize fun, hello, and everything good. We have a candidate for class president that must signify everything great about being a member of the junior class, and I have a campaign idea to make this happen."

It was clear from the start that Mr. Connors was not just enjoying knitting in with the tribe and Lefky, but he wanted to be a part of the campaign, the plan to make Owl the next president of the junior class. So Joe Connors, owner of the Sweet Shop, offered up a strategy for the tribe.

Give a hoot

Connors began, "The real purpose of this idea must be kept quiet. The details must stay in the tribe and a few of my wait staff here at the Sweet Shop. I will have printed Sweep Shop coupons. The purpose of the coupon will be to arouse support for Owl."

Mr. Connors showed the tribe a stretch of the coupon. The coupon will read,

SWEET SHOP COUPON

Good for half off the cost of
one cherry Coke
or
one root beer float
when presented at the Sweet Shop.

This coupon MUST BE accompanied by the
purchaser's yelled "HOOOOOT."

(Purchase with yelled HOOOOT must be made
before the junior class elections are held.)

Chapter 24

Coupons to Ballots

As Lefky had figured, the three teachers he chose for Owl to request to sign his nomination form, accented by the presentation of a white rose, each happily applied their signature to Owl's form. At the end of the school day on Friday, the final slate was announced and posted before the front steps of the high school, at the top of the west end of the courtyard. Almost instantly, the courtyard became a swarming mass of chatter as students read the list of candidates for junior class officers and engaged in a higher decibel level of conversation than the usual courtyard banter.

The slate listed Bonita "Bonnie" Bentz running for junior class president versus some guy, George Owelowski. This was the first time anyone had run against her since elementary school. As anticipated, Robert Ragsdale was slated as an unopposed candidate for class vice president. No surprise here as Cathy Reynolds was once again unopposed for class secretary; however, for the office of junior class treasurer, there were two candidates listed, Michael Waterfield and Paula Anderson, both honor students who had run against each other for the same office in last year's sophomore class election.

As Lefky had predicted, there was a buzz around the candidacy of George "Owl" Owelowski. The first question on everyone's lips was, who the hell is George Owelowski? It didn't take long before the answer to that question came back. "One of Lefky's clan."

Instantly, George, a.k.a. Owl, was more than a curiosity. Everyone wanted to know who he was and why he would run against Bonnie Bentz, considered a foregone conclusion to win the election for class president.

As a too-deep crowd stood fast in front of the poster board that rested on a large metal easel, listing the slate of candidates on the courtyard's west end, chatter centered on the races for class treasurer and class president. Mired in the middle of the crowd around the slate of candidates was Bonnie Bentz herself. With hands on her hips and a stern grimace, she spoke candidly with those around her, "This George candidate is an absolute joke. He is a nobody."

Myron Alston, standing next to Bonnie, asserted, "This is some kind of gag Lefky is pulling. Wait and see. Don't worry about Owl running against you. He is one of those guys who hangs around Lefkowitz. You'll win. This is like running unopposed. Owl running for class president? This is just for laughs, but it should be interesting to see what Lefky has up his sleeve."

Chapter 25

The Campaign Begins

From the moment of the posting of the slate of candidates, there was only one week to unleash a campaign for Owl. Lefky knew they needed help create a campaign that would reach every junior class member. With four hundred Sweet Shop coupons in hand, made possible by the generosity and support of Sweet Shop owner Joe Connors, Lefky enlisted the help of five junior girls, including the always energetic Joey Galacious. Joey Galacious, Jane Brady, Karen Gathers, Carla Russo, and Kelly Zocco gathered at the Sweet Shop at Lefky's behest for a briefing session the day after the candidates' release. Similar to how Mr. Connors was almost giddy about being included in one of Lefky's schemes, the girls he asked to help with the campaign were excited to help but expressed some trepidation that they did not want to do anything illegal or get into any trouble in school. Parenthetically, it seemed that the five girls were attracted to the element of risk and danger that accompanied anything to do with Arthur Lefkowitz. Lefky named this new campaign group the Owlettes.

Sitting in the back booth customarily reserved for Lefky's tribe, the five girls received a humorless, carefully detailed plan of what each needed to do for the campaign of Owl. Lefky explained that this was a serious campaign and that Owl *must* be elected.

He stressed that there is nothing nefarious or comical about Owl's candidacy, so they can never giggle or make negative comments when classmates ask about Owl. As a demonstration of loyalty, he stressed to the Owlettes that if anyone they speak with chooses to say anything derogatory about Owl, they are to walk away. "Do not shrug or do anything that implies you agree with them or don't care."

Now to the tactics. Each member of the Owlettes was given twenty-five half-off coupons for cherry Cokes or root beer floats at the Sweet Shop. Each voucher was signed on the back by Sweet Shop owner, Joe Connors, to prove the genuineness of the coupon. A coupon is only given to a junior who gives a "hoot."

The Owlettes and the tribe are to "buttonhole" as many juniors in the hallways and cafeteria during school hours and circulate through the courtyard before and after school. Each of them is responsible for approaching any of the 223 members of the junior class and politely, with a smile, asking the person, "Please give me a *hoot* for Owl."

"If the junior smiles back or gives you a 'hoot,' no matter how loud, you are to say, 'How would you like a half-off coupon for the Sweet Shop?'

"If the person gives you any positive response, give them a Sweet Shop coupon and explain, 'This offer is only good if you give a loud "hoot" for Owl at the Sweet Shop before the day of the balloting.'"

Now armed with the Sweep Shop coupons, the campaign began in earnest on the Monday before the Friday when the campaign speeches and balloting would take place. While Bonnie Bentz and her younger sister, a sophomore, were taping up eight-by-eleven paper campaign signs on the few allowable spaces for posters around the school that stated, "BONNIE IS BEST, keep the Owl in his nest," Lefky decided to conduct a person-to-person campaign, so no time was wasted on preparing or hanging candidate posters for Owl.

Besides, there were too few permissible areas where signs could be hung in the school. The tribe and the Owlettes spread their enthusiasm and charm all over the hallways and courtyard of the high school, resulting in intermittent "hoots" from students. Even students who weren't juniors thought it a "cool" thing to do and would offer a "hoot" in the hallways, some with a creative flair, such as the senior who yodeled "HOOT." As the five days of campaigning wore on, the hallways became a constant bane of "hoots," prompting some teachers to ask the hooters to quell their hooting.

Chapter 26

Owl, The Makeover

One of the waitresses at the Sweet Shop, Roxanne, was an aspiring beautician who took classes at night, working on getting training and certification to be a hairdresser/cosmetologist. With seemingly everyone into the act with the latest Lefky scheme, Roxie agreed to do a makeover on Owl. The day after Owl got his nomination form into the Faculty Leadership Council and was slated, Roxie went to work on Owl's "look." She cut his hair from a straggly, long, dirty-looking mess into a high, tight haircut that gave him a look of maturity.

Roxie's father, Malcolm, owned a men's clothier on Center Street. Roxie explained to her father what they were doing on behalf of a young man who "needed a break," and Malcolm's Men Shop brought Owl in, escorted by Roxie, and did a complete clothing "redo" that included shoes, over-the-calf socks, ties, dress shirts, and two sport jackets. She was remarkably deft at asking "Daddy" to do anything for her; such is the magic of some fathers and their daughters. The makeover on Owl took less than two days.

With three days remaining before the campaign speeches and voting, Owl wore his new attire daily to school, generating greater interest in the candidate George Owelowski. Predictably, the girls noticed, notably Linda Rosens. Looking in his eyes, the entrancing Rosens told Owl that he was handsome and getting close to Owl, whispered, "Hoot, hoot, hoot."

Having yet to even experience a date in high school, Owl was awkward in how he reacted to the kind words of Linda. On Tuesday of election week, Linda said the words Owl wanted to hear, "Meet you on the courtyard after school?"

Owl could only respond as most students did during this week of the election, "Hoot."

Owl was feeling as presidential as he looked, and every minute of the weeklong campaign brought him closer to the hour of his speech that he practiced in the back room of the Sweet Shop and at home tirelessly.

Chapter 27

Courtyard Campaigning

Monday, the first day of campaigning, the courtyard was brimming with members of the junior class, all clamoring with talk of Friday's impending election of officers. The six candidates circulated through the throngs of students, and the Owlettes were causing quite a stir as they handed out half-off coupons for the Sweet Shop, insisting on a required "hoot."

It was quite a novelty to all as a campaign activity as every student wanted to get their hands on one of those coupons, and exclaiming a hearty "HOOT" was a small price to pay.

As students began to break down into smaller groups, over in the southernmost corner of the courtyard was a candidate for office, Robert Ragsdale and his girlfriend, Carol Saphora, generally considered the most attractive girl in the school. Their conversation was no model of congeniality.

Carol was animated with pointed gestures that accompanied her harsh words. She had shoved her face under the chin of the taller Robert with her left index finger in his chest. Carol was laying into Robert in an unbridled, accusatory rebuke that he was cheating on her with Julia Derigg. Robert asked her to quiet down, that it was embarrassing them, but Carol was unrelenting. The other students who just happened to be gathered in that corner of the courtyard tried to act as though they weren't listening, but all were tuned in to every word, especially this being one of the more notable twosomes in the school.

Robert tried to calm Carol down, speaking softly, "Babe, Julia Derigg is just my tutor. You know that."

Carol would not let up, offering acrimonious comments, "Listen, big shot ... Mr. Basketball Star ... class officer, *I've seen the way she looks at you.* Don't you dare tell me that mute girl is just your tutor."

With finality, Carol reached to the lapel of her waist jacket and ripped off the varsity pin that Robert had given her last summer as a sign that they were "going steady." With one snap of her wrist, she threw the pin at Robert. Unfortunately, the angry Carol kept up the verbal barrage as Robert stood and took all the incoming palaver that Carol pilled on him.

Owl was standing at mid-courtyard and heard the commotion. He immediately excused himself from a conversation, in which he was so engaged, and walked through the muddle of students to the heated discussion of Carol and Robert. At the same time, Diane Deere, a friend of Carol's, stepped between Carol and Robert and implored Carol to "simmer down and don't embarrass yourself further."

Diane was able to talk Carol down from the angry diatribe she was leveling at Robert. Diane then took Carol by the arm and directed her to the sidewalk of Main Street, a mere fifteen feet away. Together, arm in arm, Diane and Carol walked toward Center Street, perhaps for a visit to the Sweet Shop.

Robert was close to tears after the dressing down at the hand of Carol as Owl came up to him and suggested they go for a walk, in the opposite direction of Diane and Carol. Owl hardly knew Robert but was bothered by the nasty words directed at him by Carol and the humiliation that Robert must have felt. Owl reached down and picked up the varsity pin Carol had flung at Robert and tried to hand it back to Robert. The tall Robert held the gold pin in his hand, looked at it for a moment, and then gave it back to Owl with these words, "You hold it for me. You never know you might find the girl of your dreams and have nothing to give her and you can use this pin."

Owl and Robert walked up South Main Street, along the path of historic houses. After some many steps of silence, Robert broke the ice and asked, "May I call you George, or are you only Owl?"

With those words from Robert's lips, Owl felt even worse for Robert but did as he was asked and tucked the varsity pin in his navy blue blazer.

With a touch of laughter, George smiled and said, "Other than my parents, no one has called me George in some time. Even my teachers refer to me as Owl. Robert? I would be honored for you to call me George."

With extended hand, Robert looked at his fellow candidate for junior class office and declared, "George ... my name is Robert. It is a privilege to know the next president of the junior class."

George shook Robert's hand and stated, "It is a pleasure to know you, Robert Ragsdale, and it will be an honor to serve the junior class as officers ... together."

With that handshake, Owl, George, suggested, "Let's get back to the courtyard. There must be a challenge or two we need to overcome together."

Laughter ensued, and it seemed to both young men that a new dawn had risen for them.

Chapter 28

The Speech—*A Hoot*

After the meeting of the tribe at the Sweet Shop that chose Owl as their candidate for class president, Lefky immediately got to work on Owl's speech and some strategy to help Owl, who was not only reticent but also never had made a speech in his life, except a required oral report or two for social studies.

Lefky needed more than a bit of help to write Owl's speech, so he reached out to a senior member of the editorial staff of the school newspaper, Duane Dueland, whom Lefky nicknamed Dweeb. He was talented with words; he could keep his mouth shut, and Lefky let Dweeb borrow his car on dates.

Before the Friday of the scheduled campaign speeches and balloting session for junior class officers, the six candidates for all four offices met with Mr. McCain in his office to draw lots for who would speak in what order. As with everything pertaining to the election, Lefky instructed Owl to choose to speak after Bonnie, *if* he had a choice. Now that it was strictly a matter of chance as to who spoke in what order, Owl just wanted to get the speech over and rid himself of this sickly feeling in his gut.

Mr. McCain turned his black fedora hat upside down and dropped in pieces of paper, numbered lots, 1–6. The candidates reached into the hat in alphabetical order. Bonita Bentz drew the first lot and pulled out no. 5.

She glared at Owl and said, "That's exactly what I wanted." When it was time for Owl to pick a lot from the hat, he grabbed no. 6, so he would speak right after Bonnie. Owl wondered what Lefky would think of the speakers' order.

Per plan, Owl met with the tribe at the Sweet Shop right after the meeting with Mr. McCain. Upon opening the door of the Sweet Shop, the tribe was waiting, and they rose from their seats at the booth and jointly screamed a collective, "HOOT."

After hearing the news that Owl would be the last speaker at the campaign speeches and balloting session, Lefky was elated.

Lefky had given Owl his campaign speech two days earlier. Lefky didn't want Owl to memorize it. He wanted Owl to say it slowly and with power. Owl spent hours practicing the speech out loud in his bedroom and during that time, had become enamored with the idea that he could be a "good president" by caring about the students in the junior class.

It came to him with every repetition of every sentence in the speech. "Be the kind of leader every member of the junior class will be proud to call you their president."

Absorbed in the words of the speech written by Lefky and Dweeb, Owl sincerely wanted to win. It was just that this speech-giving was almost terrifying.

Unknown to Owl, Lefky had built in a strategy that would make the speech one for the ages. The Owlettes—Joey, Jane, Donna, Carla, and Sandy—had been spreading the goodwill of Owl, campaigning for him with the use of the Sweet Shop coupons in the hallways and on the courtyard since Owl was officially declared a candidate for president, but they had one more vital task.

Each of the Owlettes was supplied with three copies of the actual speech Owl would deliver at the podium. They were each asked to find three members of the class they could trust and charm that person into helping support Owl in the following manner:

As Owl delivered his speech, each student they enlisted was armed with an exact word-for-word copy of the address.

In their copies of the speech, when Owl got to specific phrases, there were "prompts," triggering the person to yell out a prolonged "Hoot!"

The Owlettes had done their best to find a cadre of students who would fall in with their plan to *hoot for Owl* during his speech. Surprisingly, the reaction to their request for "hooting" was met with great enthusiasm. The idea of overtly showing this kind of spirit for a candidate during a speech was exciting to the students who were asked to hoot for Owl.

Chapter 29

Campaign Speeches

The morning of the day of the campaign speeches and balloting for junior class officers had arrived. The six candidates for office were seated in the front row of the auditorium as the junior class homerooms piled into the auditorium's lower seating. Class members held some posters for their favorite candidate, but some faculty members found it interesting that those posters featured candidates who ran unopposed.

Bonnie Bentz was sitting next to Owl as the candidates were seated in order of their appearance. Before the proceedings began with the drone of the muffled voices of the audience in the background, Bonnie leaned toward George, Owl, and without looking at him, muttered, "I know this is some kind of joke that Lefky put you up to. You know you can't win. You should be embarrassed."

Owl turned to look at Bonnie. "I want to serve our class. Let's see who is embarrassed when the day is done."

Instantly, Owl felt a sense of pride in the words he had just spoken and a lift in his confidence.

Mr. McCain stepped to the podium and explained the rules for campaign speeches and that the candidates for each office would go in the order of a lottery previously drawn from a hat. Then the candidates walked up onto the stage one by one and presented their speeches not to exceed two minutes. Unopposed, Kathy Reynolds was first, and she approached her speech in that fashion with a very casual approach. Her first words were, "Isn't this fun? Wow, we are juniors already."

With the preparation he had put into his speech and all the plans and contributions of Lefky, Mr. Connors, his staff, and the Owlettes, he wondered how committed to anything Kathy could be.

Robert Ragsdale was second. He was tall and handsome, and rumor had it that his girlfriend, Carol, the best-looking girl in the school, in Owl's opinion, was about to give Robert the "brown helmet." Robert, a talented athlete, talked about using the lessons he had learned on the basketball court to lead the junior class. Owl wondered how shooting a basketball might help the junior class, but Robert was a good speaker, smiling, and looked comfortable. He didn't have anyone running against him, so all he had to do in his speech was not make any mistakes.

After the next two candidates, Michael Waterfield, who spoke like he wanted to be a comedian, and Paula Anderson, whose final words in her speech were "And you know I can do the job, right?" it was Bouncing Bonnie's turn.

As Bonnie was introduced, she got a fair amount of applause. Upon reaching the podium, she unfolded a piece of three-holed notebook paper and began, "And how are you all doing? You all know me. I have been your president for a long time and haven't heard any complaints. You know I am an honor student and attend as many school events as any of you. What more can I say?"

As Owl watched Bonnie and listened to her speech, his focus was clearly on his speech and performing it exactly how Lefky and the tribe prepared him. Then in a twinkling, the focus of his thoughts was yanked right from under him as Bonnie Bentz spoke this sentence, "How can any of you sit there and even consider voting for someone named after a smelly bird? How embarrassing would that be to say your class president is ... Owl."

Lefky, seated in an aisle seat with his homeroom, approximately twenty feet away from the stage, was incensed, inflamed with those words. He wanted to react and did all he could to contain his rage. Teachers and students assembled in the auditorium gasped at the insensitivity of Bonnie Bentz, but no rule of protocol was violated, so no one responded, even Principal McCain.

As she left the stage, Mr. McCain passed Bonnie and quietly said to her, "Was that necessary?"

Some students wondered what Owl would say or do in response. There was a feeling of suspense in the hall as McCain introduced the final candidate for office. "Members of the junior class, a candidate for class president, George Owelowski."

Maybe because of what Bonnie Bentz had just said or possibly because the junior students were required to sit through five speeches, but as Owl strode to the stage, there was a confluence of "hoots" and applause.

Per Lefky's instructions, Owl, clothed in a navy blue blazer, heather-gray slacks, black Oxford shoes, and a teal tie, approached the pentagon podium with molded columns carved in the rounded arches to the sides. Carrying a file folder, Owl laid it on the highly polished upper shelf and took out his speech, mounted on heavy cover stock paper.

He raised his head, looking over the junior class audience, paused a few seconds, and performed the speech just as he rehearsed it home alone and with the tribe:

My Fellow Members of the Junior Class,

We stand on the threshold of the greatest days of our high school years. (yell: HOOT)

At first, the twenty or so students in possession of Owl's speech yelled out a HOOT sound as their copy of the address indicated them to do so with the typed the words "yell: HOOT," but it didn't take long before a growing number of class members joined in the fun in the apparent responsive speech of Owl.

We have an opportunity to be the best junior class in school history. (yell: HOOT)

106

Fellow juniors, that doorway to this opportunity will only open if we say no to the "same old, same old."

You all know what the "same old is." That's reelecting the same tired candidates, most of whom have been running for your class offices, unopposed, year after year. (yell: HOOT)

Our junior class deserves better. Our junior class deserves a choice. (yell: HOOT)

Do you think anything will improve by washing, drying, and folding the same officers for another year?

This is our junior year, the most important year of our high school career.

I say we deserve better than doing everything or, in some cases, doing nothing *the same way.* (yell: HOOT, HOOT, HOOT)

The junior class deserves the best leadership we can provide, rather than the same old "Let's do the prom the same as last year," or most importantly, "Let's do the annual First Lighting of the Lantern Gala as we have always done it."

I say, we can do better. (yell: HOOT)

Some of you call me Owl, and that's acceptable, but I will not hide from my responsibility to serve you. You, our junior class, is my top priority. (yell: HOOT)

Most importantly, I want to be your president, a president you *can count on, committed to improving all* we *do together.* (yell: HOOT)

The junior class deserves a choice to do better—make that choice!

Fellow members of the junior class, don't you deserve a choice? (yell: HOOT)

I am George Owelowski, and I wish to serve you as your class president.

You now have a choice—a leadership choice.

In less than one hour, you will cast your ballot on that choice.

How will you vote? (yell: HOOT, HOOT, HOOT, HOOT)

Chapter 30

The Vote

Immediately following the final speeches of the junior class office candidates, the voting process began.

Mr. McCain and the Faculty Leadership Council had organized this year's voting process. Mr. McCain was well aware that Arthur Lefkowitz had been a presence in the previous week of campaigning and surmised that Lefky was probably behind all the "hooting" that was shouted between classes and in the cafeteria. For McCain, the potential for a Lefky ruse was enough to put in some safeguards to head off any possible improper activity or, as McCain put it, "Lefky hanky-panky" in the balloting.

Heretofore, Mr. McCain took to the podium at the conclusion of the speeches and announced a new procedure for casting ballots for the election of officers.

1. Each homeroom will leave the auditorium, one at a time, exiting through the rear entrance doors. There, three stations are set up with a member of the faculty council at each to register each student listed on an alphabetical list of junior class members.
2. Once registered, each junior will be given a clipboard with a ballot and asked to circle the name of one candidate for each office. The completed ballot clipboard will be returned to the faculty council teacher.
3. All ballots will be checked and deposited in a cardboard box under Mr. McCain's supervision.

4. After all members of the junior class attending the campaign speeches have completed and submitted their ballots to a faculty council member, they are to return to their homeroom and subsequently be dismissed to the next regularly scheduled class.

5. All ballots will be counted, and the results will be announced and posted on the courtyard at 2:45 p.m.

Chapter 31

Waiting for The Outcome

For George Owelowski, a quiet young man who had never known the tension of competition, the deflation of disappointment, or the elation of victory, the four hours of waiting to hear the results of the election was a swirling admixture of emotions. It was all new for the one nicknamed Owl, and George didn't want to give it up when the election results were posted.

Only three weeks ago, George was just Owl, a diligent student who got a thrill by being around Lefky and his tribe. Now, for the first time, he wanted something. He really wanted to be class president. He found a new joy in looking good in his blazer and tie. He felt ten feet tall when Linda Rosens stood before him and talked with her eyes, not needing words to make him feel special.

Bonnie Bentz felt as confident as everyone in her circle of friends told her that she couldn't lose, especially not to the skinny kid, Owl. She went about her business after the balloting, doing what she always did in class and accepting the congratulations of her friends on what they all expected to be another year of Bonnie as class president.

For Lefky, the class election was the most out in the open he had been in memory. Ordinarily, Lefky would wheel and deal behind the scenes, pulling the strings of some harmless prank. This time he knew he had "come out of the cold," publicly planning a candidate's campaign.

During the four hours between the speeches and the posting of the election results, Lefky thought about the balloting process and how he might have connived the election under different circumstances. This time, for all the right reasons, Lefky had decided to step into the fray and be a part of the process, and his candidate might just win this thing.

Chapter 32

A Forever Surprise

As the final minutes of this Friday school day ticked off the clock, students and faculty anxiously awaited the announcement of the junior class officer election results. As the dismissal bells sounded, students exited the school, streaming onto the courtyard, many jockeying for position near the stairs where the posting would be placed.

Mr. McCain and two faculty council members had counted the ballots, limiting the number of staff who knew the results. Mr. McCain's secretary prepared a large poster board with her handwritten names of the newly elected junior class officers written in three-inch letters.

With a white covering over the poster board listing the new junior class officers, Mr. McCain and Mrs. Loomis set up the easel in place. A smile upon his face, he looked over the hundred or so students jammed together on the west end of the courtyard. Without a megaphone or any electronic device, Mr. McCain barked, "And now, members of the junior class, I proudly post your class officers for this year."

Removing the white paper covering, there were immediate gasps and hoots as George Owelowski had, indeed, outvoted Bonita Bentz for the office of junior class president.

George, Owl, was tucked into the assembled crowd, standing alongside Lefky and a few members of the Owlettes. Lefky, overjoyed, yelled out to the crowd, "Now give me a real HOOT!"

And the courtyard and a portion of Main Street shook to a thunderous collective HOOT.

As posted, the new junior class officers were listed:

George Owelowski, President
Robert Ragsdale, Vice President
Kathy Reynolds, Secretary
Paula Anderson, Treasurer

Chapter 33

Aftermath

Predictably, Bouncing Bonnie was reduced to tears upon learning of the balloting results. Her friends tried to console her, but the shock of her upending to Owl was just too much to take. One of the faculty advisers to the junior class, Gail Emhoff, who was there on the courtyard, equally surprised by the posted results, attempted to comfort Bonnie. Still, the stunning defeat was just too much for Bonnie to swallow.

Each member of the tribe felt a sense of legitimacy after years of "razing hell" in covert pranks. Owl accepted raucous congratulatory hugs and messing-up-his-hair gestures by Bando, Arse, and Lefky. Lefky looked for Bonnie, wanting to approach her and take his pound of verbal flesh after her pompous insult of him a few weeks ago. For whatever personal reason, Lefky felt sorry for the now-dethroned class president.

Linda Rosens joyfully came up to Owl, threw her arms around his neck, and with her eyes aglow looking into his, sarcastically asked, "Well now, Owl, what is the first thing you will do as president of our class?"

With a broad smile, Owl thought for a second and calmly asked, "I wanted to inquire if I might kiss you … just once?"

The beautiful Linda felt a distinctive emotion stirring in her heart and with a giggle, said, "Mr. President … George, I would be honored if you would kiss me, but would you mind delaying that kiss for a while?"

As with everything in that moment, it was all too much, and there would be time for all things.

On the fringe of the courtyard stood Mr. Connors, looking proud. Lefky, seeing the owner of the Sweet Shop, approached him with a hug and a few words. "Joe, there is no way we could have done this without you. If it wasn't for your coupons, we couldn't have sucked in all these juniors to vote for Owl."

Then it hit Mr. Connors. "Oh my god … I forgot about the coupons. I better get back. We are liable to have a mob scene at the Sweet Shop."

Trotting off down Main Street to his shop a few blocks away, it occurred to Joe that he may be unable to accommodate all these coupon holders.

Chapter 34

The Sweet (Shop) Celebration

The crowd dissipated from the joyous courtyard, making their way to the Sweet Shop or home. By 4:00 p.m., the Sweet Shop was a continuous scream of "hoots" as the coupons were honored even though the election was over. Throughout the evening, the wait staff tried their best to keep up with the preparation of root beer floats and the long-spoon mixing of cherry Cokes.

With students and the regular customers crowded into every booth, the topic of conversation was how the election results turned out, more specifically, how could Bonnie Bentz have lost. It seemed impossible. At 9:30 p.m., Mr. McCain, the principal, and his wife, Muriel, came into the Sweet Shop for ice cream to top off their Friday evening at the movies down at the Wilkinson Theater. The Sweet Shop wait staff had put in a long day, and Joe Connors, the owner, had been in a constant state of hustle since they opened. One of the staff alerted Joe that Principal McCain was in the shop; Joe promptly went over to Mr. McCain's booth to welcome him.

Joe mentioned to Mr. McCain that it must have been hectic at the school with the junior class elections. Joe added, "And you had an upset in your president's election, didn't you? All the kids have been talking about it."

Because of fatigue or a loose moment in talking with another adult, Mr. McCain candidly stated, "It wasn't really an upset. Between you and me, the vote wasn't close all that close."

With that information, Mr. Connors wanted to ask more about the vote spread but was happy to have a piece of information to tantalize Lefky.

To Joe Connors's surprise, even though 150 half-off coupons were turned in with their required "hoot," the Sweet Shop did pretty well at the cash register last week.

A Time to Lead

Lefky prepared Owl for the campaign and gave him everything George needed to be victorious. As George laid his head on the pillow at midnight, he realized all the people he needed to thank for this winning election, but a more significant issue was floating in his head: *Now I have to lead the class. How do I do that?*

George remembered the almost kiss of Linda Rosens and wondered what that might have been like. It was a vision he would keep close to his heart for days to come.

Monday, this next Monday, I shall begin to lead my class. George pledged to God that starting Monday, *I shall begin to help make this year's First Lighting of the Lantern Gala the best gala in history.* With those thoughts, he said, "Linda, I shall kiss you."

Soon sleep would come over George, Owl, and things in his life would never be the same.

Chapter 35

Julia and The Vice President

Amid the celebratory spirit that reigned over the courtyard on this day of the announcement of the newly elected junior class officers, Julia Derigg appeared on the edge of the courtyard. Julia had always avoided the courtyard and any place where groups of students gathered, wanting to avoid the hurtful comments about her and her inability to speak.

Julia's presence on the courtyard was solely to see the young man she continued to tutor in Algebra II, Robert Ragsdale. For almost a month, Julia had committed her daily lunch period to instructing Robert at some table in a corner, away from those who would make fun of her muteness. Given the isolation she has endured by choice and circumstance brought about by her inability to speak, the time she spent with Robert was more than with anyone she had ever known other than her parents and grandmother.

Tucked in her heart was a growing fondness for Robert that had only been shared with her grandmother. The handsome and popular Robert had this day been elected to another year as junior class vice president, and Julia knew she had to try and at least see his triumph on the courtyard. The lovely and diminutive Julia tried to remain away from the throngs of students. Still, in her desire to catch a glimpse of Robert, who was somewhere in the middle of the mass of students, she warily made her way around the fringe of the courtyard.

119

Nearing the edge of the sidewalk on Main Street, trying to avoid being noticed, suddenly, Robert was standing to her left.

There was instant joy in her heart as she looked up at the much-taller Robert. Not wanting her gestures to be misinterpreted by anyone, she reached in her purse for her pad and pen. She wrote, "So happy ... you're the VP."

Robert tried to hug her. Julia waved her hands in front of her, indicating, "Please don't," but Julia wanted his embrace. Julia wrote on her pad again. "We have work to do, big midterm next week."

"Must we talk about that now? Everyone is having such a good time," observed Robert.

Julia looking past Robert, noticed Carol Saphora. She was scowling at them.

Julia wrote on her pad, "Not everyone!"

Tomorrow was Saturday, and Julia asked, "Do you want to come to my home at 10:00 a.m.?"

Robert nodded and responded, "Are we just factoring, or shall I prepare to perform something for your grandmother and your mother? You told me your grandmother finds rain very romantic. How about I play Chopin's Raindrop Prelude, Opus 28, No. 15?"

"Algebra II, chapters 1–18, *only*," Julia frantically wrote on her pad, ripped the page off it, and gave it to Robert.

Feeling odd being seen with Robert with his girlfriend, Carol, not far from them, looking daggers at them, Julia gave a wave of goodbye and headed off to the walk along Main Street and home. Robert spoke softly, "See you tomorrow. Thanks for talking to me."

Julia could not have known that Carol and Robert's relationship might be over after their recent nasty tiff and with Carol having given Robert back his varsity pin.

Chapter 36

A Time to Think

As with all celebratory events, there is a "day after" when a calm fills the air and one wonders if what occurred the day before actually happened.

Robert decided to walk to Julia's home for his 10:00 a.m. tutoring session, sauntering up Ward Street and taking a left onto Main Street. The walk afforded him time to think, not of the previous day's election of junior class officers or the ensuing basketball season, of which so much is expected of him as the team's best returning player, but of the girl who had entered his life quite unexpectedly with one purpose in mind: to help him pass Algebra II.

Changing the pace of his strides, Robert peregrinated past the historic homes of Main Street. He pondered the events of the last few weeks, including his failures in Algebra II. In recent school years, Robert has often felt overwhelmed in math and was aware that he needed help if he had any chance to pass Algebra II. His teacher, Mr. Crampitz, could have asked any of five or six top students to help him with the course work, but Robert was convinced that Mr. Crampitz purposefully assigned a mute girl to tutor him, probably as a ploy to belittle and embarrass him. Mr. Crampitz had no use for athletics or athletes he presumed were the recipients of far too much undeserved recognition.

Julia knew little of Robert and felt no emotion or had no other motivation other than to comply with her math teacher's request. As with all school-related assignments,

Julia methodically and with seriousness of purpose instructed Robert.

Neither Robert nor Julia could have anticipated the fallout from what started as a simple tutoring arrangement assigned by Mr. Crampitz. Observing Robert with a pretty girl, albeit a mute girl, day after day during the lunch wave at some remote table, presumably for the purpose of tutoring him in math, was not acceptable to Carol Saphora, his long-standing girlfriend.

With each step that brought him nearer to Julia's home, Robert kept returning to thoughts of Carol and how much he thought he loved her. He knew he didn't do anything wrong or disloyal to Carol, but what was confounding to him was how Carol acted with so much anger, summarily terminating their relationship. He had blamed himself since Carol threw his varsity pin back at him in the courtyard, but the more he thought of Carol's act of wrath, the more he was convinced that maybe Carol just stopped wanting him as her boyfriend. Perhaps it was just that simple.

Pausing to look over his left shoulder, he stared at the tall ten-foot pole that suspended the legendary Lantern. Robert and Carol had decided to make this year's gala their once-in-a-lifetime first "Lantern kiss," in their junior year. This year's gala was to be the singular kiss moment under the Lantern for Carol and him, a long-awaited romantic kiss that prophecy had foretold would seal their love. Not that Robert and Carol hadn't kissed before, they had many times, but like many Wallingford couples of all ages, the kiss under the Lantern was to be a star-crossed twinkling shared by scores of students and adults alike. Those plans were forever dashed on the rocks of heartbreak and what might have been.

The more he looked at the Lantern, the more guilt he felt that it was his fault the relationship with Carol had broken down; however, Robert felt no emptiness or sadness, just confusion from an all-of-a-sudden moment in his young life.

Passing the Sweet Shop, just beginning to brim with excitement on this Saturday morning as parents, shopping at the stores along Center Street with their family members in tow, would succumb to the pleas of their young children for an ice cream cone with rainbow shots.

With the final few hundred yards of sidewalk before him until he reached Julia's home, Robert's thoughts returned to Julia. Washing over him was the vision of her face. There was depth in her piercing hazel eyes. From the first minutes he sat next to her, her eyes seemed to look right through him. Full of expression and meaning, Julia communicated to him with her eyes. It was all so unnerving at first, but with every tutoring session since, with every one of her glances in his direction, Robert felt something so different from anyone he had ever known. Julia's eyes talked to him. He didn't understand it, but he looked forward to every opportunity to look into her eyes.

When a young man is alone with his thoughts, they will invariably lead him to the desires of his heart. There is often internal conflict regarding right and wrong, action and procrastination. Robert was conflicted to be sure. The relationship with Carol, thought by many fellow students as one made in heaven, destined to last a lifetime, had come to a thunderous halt. He wondered whether that recent circumstance would or had already unduly influenced his growing feelings for Julia. It was all so confusing. Whom could he talk with about all this internal turmoil? Whom did he trust enough to speak from his heart? In the middle of this muddle of feelings, he laughed out loud, concluding he only wanted to talk with Julia, the object of his bewilderment.

Turning the corner to Julia's home, Robert stopped to look at her majestic house. Scanning the two-story stone abode, he anxiously looked forward to seeing her. His focus should have been on the concepts of Algebra II, but he was thoroughly distracted. How could he not be?

Upon ringing the front doorbell with its booming chimes, he stood tall with a math book clutched in his hand. Just then, the large front door opened, and standing in front of him was not Julia but her grandmother, Denise. She smiled at him, knowing of her granddaughter's affection for the lad, and summoned him to enter. The demure grandmother explained that Julia was upstairs dressing, exercising her God-given gift as a woman to be "fashionably late." Robert smiled and assured Denise that no faux pau had been committed.

As Robert and Julia's grandmother traded welcoming sentences, Denise dropped a comment on Robert that caused him to gasp. "So, Robert, have you placed your name on every girl's First Kiss Dance Card for the gala?"

Robert responded instantly, "Why no, the First Kiss Dance Cards for the gala won't be available to people for a few weeks."

"I see, Robert," stated Denise, "and you know that although you may request a dance with many girls and write your name on her dance card, you may *only* request one kiss."

Robert let out a belly laugh. "Thank you for your reminder, but I am aware of the long-abiding decree that a boy may request one and only one kiss, and it must be a first forever kiss."

The witty grandmother smiled knowingly at the handsome Robert, adding a clever rhetorical comment, "Then I am sure you are well aware of the prophecy, and I quote, 'If first kissed under the lantern, forever moonlit will be thy heart.'"

With that blast of prophecy, both laughed uncontrollably as Julia descended the stairs and hearing their words, signed to her Grandmother, "And what are my Grandmother and he who is my 'tutee' doing in the foyer?"

Chapter 37

One More Question

Joining Robert and her grandmother in the foyer, Julia signed, "What were all the giggles about?"

Grandmother Denise stated, "Little one (Julia), your friend and I were reviewing certain protocols and traditions of our community. I am sure you would not object."

With that explanation, Julia reached for Robert's left hand and led him to the sitting room, where Julia had administered his instruction the last time he came to her home.

There would be no piano playing or small talk between the tutor and the tutee. Julia had prepared fourteen mini-quizzes, covering every chapter and subchapter, and fully intended to put him through the full battery of tests on this day. With the midterm examinations this week, she had to prepare him to pass the exam.

Wasting no time, Julia began shortly after 10:00 a.m., giving Robert her handwritten declaration on teal stationery, "I hope you don't have any plans for today because you aren't leaving here until you are ready to pass Mr. Crampitz's midterm."

With those words, Julia reviewed each chapter and tested Robert with ten problem quizzes. Correcting each quiz as they went along, Julia would circle back to a chapter and test him again if Robert didn't solve eight out of ten problems correctly.

By 1:00 p.m., with no breaks or casual chat, Julia had beat his brains in with Algebra II, and still, she continued her relentless math onslaught. At 3:00 p.m., he had successfully passed all fourteen quizzes, with four he had to take twice. By this time, Robert was not in good humor, and Julia had one more test to give him. It was a twenty-problem test, which included a question from every chapter scheduled to be on the midterm. Correcting that culminating test together, Robert answered eighteen of the twenty problems correctly. Both mentally exhausted, Julia once again wrote on her pad, "Robert, you are as ready as I can make you. I know you are going to pass Mr. Crampitz's midterm. I just know it."

Robert looked into her eyes and offered a gentle smile. "Julia, how can I thank you for all you have done for me?"

In big bold letters, Julia wrote on her pad, "PASS THIS MIDTERM."

Just then, Julia's grandmother walked into the sitting room and asked, "Are you two OK? Your mother and I haven't heard a sound from this room since you started hours ago."

Looking at her grandmother, Julia signed, "Grandmother, will you do me a favor and ask Robert a question for me? My hands are too sore from writing on my pad all day."

Denise nodded, and Julia signed to her grandmother, "Please ask Robert if he has any more questions?"

Denise spoke the words to Robert that Julia had signed to her, "Robert, do you have any other questions?"

Robert looked down as if gathering his thoughts. Then slowly raising his eyes, he found the eyes of Julia seated next to him. With her grandmother opposite them, Robert pursed his lips together and took Julia's left hand with both of his.

Speaking quietly, Robert leaned forward. "Julia, I do have *one* important question."

A foot away from Robert's face, Julia made a waving gesture in front of her as if to suggest, "Well, c'mon ... ask me."

Robert took her hands into both of his, allowing his eyes to sink deeper into her eyes, and whispered, "May I have the honor to be your escort at the First Lighting of the Lantern Gala on November 2?"

Instantly, Julia's eyes became as large and round as saucers as her grandmother yelled out, "Sweet Jesus!" and exited the sitting room posthaste.

Julia welled up in tears and slowly moved her head left and right, gesturing, "NO."

She rapidly patted her fingertips to her shoulders while shaking her head, "NO," but Robert just smiled and nodded his head "yes."

Julia grabbed her pad and wrote, "What about Carol?"

"There is no more, Carol," responded Robert as he explained that they had broken up.

With tears dripping down her cheeks, Julia wrote on her pad, "You don't want *me*. You can't want *me*. *No*."

Holding her hands, his eyes never leaving hers, he spoke with the softness of raindrops falling on a rosebud's petals. Robert's lips were but inches away from Julia's right ear, and his whisper of words expressed the strings of his heart that he had never before spoken to anyone or about anyone. "Julia," he all but sang to her, "your kindness has so moved me, and I have thought of little else other than you for weeks. You have come to mean joy and happiness, and there is no one else in heaven or on earth that I would rather have on my arm ... to dance with at the gala than you."

Overwhelmed by the shockwave of Robert's request, it triggered a tidal wave of emotions that Julia had little chance of parsing in the few seconds since she had listened to his words.

Julia sought relief, separation from the moment. She didn't know what to do and could not sort out her thoughts. She grabbed her pad and wrote, "Robert, will you give me a few minutes? I need to take care of something. Please."

"Sure, go take care of whatever you need to do. I'll be here. May I use the bathroom?"

Straight away, Julia darted down the long hallway, searching for her mother or grandmother. As usual, she found them in the breakfast nook, engaged in a rather animated conversation. Her mother, Emma, was in high spirits, asking her mother, Denise, "Are you quite sure that boy asked our Julia to the gala? This is amazing."

Julia started to sign with her mother and grandmother, "What do I do? What do I do? I've never been out with a boy. I've never danced with a boy. Oh my god, what if he wants to slow-dance? I wouldn't know how to act."

Julia's mother, Emma, looking at Julia with eyebrows down, spoke in short phrases, "What is your problem? That boy is charming, talented, and nice to look at. Why would you hesitate even for a moment? Get back in there and say yes, you silly girl."

Julia went around the back of the table where Grandmother Denise was seated and fell to her knees, looking up and signing to Denise, her go-to person, when she was hurt or confused, "Grandmother, how can I say yes to him? You know kids make fun of me. They always have. I've never danced with a boy ... I have never done anything with a boy, except tutor Robert. Grandma, I can't even talk with him over the phone. I know I will embarrass him."

Denise lifted Julia to a standing position, hugged her, and softly spoke to the most important of things, "Julia, do you like Robert?"

Julia peered into her grandmother's face, signing with a smile, "You know I do."

Emma, Julia's mother, responded, "You like? I mean, *you* really 'like' Robert?"

Julia nodded and with a pixie grin, signed, "I better get back to Robert. He has been sitting there alone for ten minutes."

Denise raised her index finger to her lips and asked, "How do you plan to answer, Robert?"

Julia signed, "Grandmother, look at me. I can't even answer a boy I like."

Her mother, Emma, fought back the tears, hurting for her daughter.

Denise smiled in adoration of Julia, suggesting, "Honey, teach him to sign. You'll know what to do."

Julia reentered the sitting room where Robert patiently waited. Robert asked again, "Julia, will you go with me to the First Lighting of the Lantern Gala?"

Julia took Robert's right hand and made it into a fist. With both of her hands, she moved his fist up and down as one would nod. Robert didn't understand and looked perplexed. Julia wrote one last time for today on her pad, "I am answering you. My first lesson to you in 'signing.'"

Julia made a fist with her left hand and moved it in the same fashion as she did with Robert's fist. On her pad, she wrote, "Robert, this (the fist nod) means ... *yes*."

With his heart thumping, Robert looked into her face, raised his fist, and for the first time, signed, "Yes."

Julia and Robert wanted to hug the other but refrained with joyous smiles donning their faces.

Robert asked, "It is getting late. I've been here for hours, but would your mother and grandmother like me to play something for them?"

Julia rushed off to get her mother and grandmother and bring them to the piano room. Julia signed to her mother, "Ask Robert to perform the Raindrop Prelude, Opus 28, Number 15 by Chopin."

Upon arriving at the piano room, Denise was the first to speak. "So I understand that you have asked to escort Julia to the Lantern gala," referencing their conversation in the foyer upon his arrival at their home on this day. "Does this mean that you plan to write your name repeatedly on Julia's dance card?"

With no hesitation, Robert signed, "YES," as Denise unleashed one of her patented unrestrained chortles.

Robert took his place on the leather bench seat before the Steinway baby grand piano. "Mrs. Derigg, is there anything I might try to play for you?"

Emma inquired, "Robert can you play Chopin's Raindrop Prelude, Opus 28, Number 15?"

Signing "yes" with his nodding right fist, a beaming Julia returned the "yes" sign.

With the end of the Chopin piece, Julia escorted Robert to the door. She was inclined to kiss him goodbye, and Robert was of a similar mind, but they only touched each other's hands, and Robert left with these words to her, "I will pass this midterm for you. I will make you proud to call me *your escort* to the gala."

With Julia's heart all a flutter, she watched Robert walking away along Main Street until he was well past the Hall Mansion.

Chapter 38

Will You Take My Arm?

An ancient nursery rhyme takes place in a tiny floral area, a "dell," where animals match up with other animals and inanimate objects under the guise "someone takes someone or something." It is a great little poem for children to learn words and names of things, but it also demonstrates how easy it is to be drawn into a relationship of various duration. The rhyme ends with the illustration of someone or something standing alone. All this is mildly reflective of the manner in which a high school boy will approach a young lady, requesting her to accompany him to a dance or a prom.

A significant aspect of the wildly popular annual gala within the community and high school is that almost everyone of every age wants to be there. With all the buildup and excitement of the gala, little children ask their parents to be included and allowed to attend, and some do. Most townspeople, enchanted by the pomp and circumstance and historical relevance, view the gala as a must-attend event every year, but for one and all, it is a see-and-be-seen extravaganza that harkens in the holiday season.

For the high school students, the First Lighting of the Lantern Gala is the ultimate coming-out party, not to be missed unless hospitalized or under lock and key.

With but a month to go before the gala on November 2, the hallways of the school and courtyard were satiated with subtle overtures by young men testing the waters of the receptibility of young ladies should he request the honor of her company at

131

the gala. Indeed, most girls were not shy in their advances to some boys, suggesting a degree of encouragement should the young man ask to escort them to the gala. There were dating couples in the student body, making it easy to complete the dialogue of "May I escort you to the gala?" "Are you going to ask me to the gala?" "Do you want to go with me to the gala?"

In the confines of the school society, the narrow hallways, classrooms, and the larger gathering areas of the cafeteria, gymnasium, auditorium, and for Wallingford, the courtyard allows for almost instant recognition of one another. Most everyone is known to everyone else, so the only remaining component of a boy escorting a girl to the gala is in the asking, "May I have the privilege of your company?"

For the junior class, the process of a boy asking a girl to be his date for the gala starts in late September and early October.

Once the junior class elections conclude, the courtyard is the fertile ground to discover who likes whom, who wants to date whom, and who can tolerate whom, as no one wants to be left at home during the gala.

Described best as the "social butterfly period" by teachers, the fact-finding process of who is dating whom and who likes whom are critical pieces of information for most boys who do not want to risk feeling embarrassed by asking a girl to the gala and being turned down. Youthful male ego being what it is, a boy can get bruised up pretty well with a quick turned down or, in some cases, a hearty laugh by a girl when she is asked to the gala by someone she feels is totally unacceptable.

A year ago, one short inobtrusive boy who was involved in a lot of organizations and activities in the high school, although few seemed to notice the lad even existed, was known to have asked eight different girls to the gala, including a non-English-speaking foreign-exchange student and was summarily told by one and all NO!

Parenthetically, no one would ever consider showing up to the gala without an escort. Hence, the gala was a time, often the first time, for many young men to formally approach a young woman for a date, but this was no ordinary date.

The newly elected junior class president George "Owl" Owelowski, having never had a date with a girl, was more than concerned about the challenge of finding a girl to escort to the gala. During the campaign, one girl had been so kind to him, Linda Rosens. George found himself thinking about her a lot during the campaign, like no other girl he had known. Here was this beautiful girl, one of the popular girls in the school, talking and smiling at him. From the first time Linda squared up to him face-to-face on the courtyard, he was enthralled by her perfect features. Her blue eyes glistened, and she seemed to hang on to his every word. Linda was the first girl he considered asking to the gala. After the first meeting of the gala cabinet, George figured he better ask someone soon before there was no one left to ask.

After the final bell on a drizzly Tuesday afternoon, he walked briskly across the courtyard and onto Main Street, intending to get along to the Sweet Shop, where he would see the members of Lefky's tribe, of which he was still one. A voice cried out, "George, George, wait up." It was Linda Rosen. With the soft rain falling with only the hood of Linda's rain jacket to protect her, George's hair was getting damp. Linda smiled and looking into his eyes, ribbed, "Well, Owl, you better get out of the rain, or your feathers will get soaked."

They laughed as instant inspiration came over him. Neither seemed to mind the October rain as George stood before Linda with dripping hair and bade the right words to come from his mouth. "Linda, would you permit me the privilege of taking you to the First Lighting of the Lantern Gala?"

There, he asked. He asked a beautiful girl to go out with him.

Linda pushed her rain hood back, exposing her blond hair to the rain. She lifted her head and drew closer to Owl, to George. Peering into his eyes, Linda asked, "Are you sure you want to lead the 'first dance' of the gala with me?"

George had forgotten all about the junior class president's ritual of leading off the night's first dance. There was another thing he had never done—dance with a girl. George rolled his eyes as Linda pressed on, "Well, Mr. President, do you want to take back your offer to escort me to the gala?"

George shot back, "No. Do you want to go with me?"

Linda smiled a magnificent grin. "George, there is no one I'd rather go with ... than you."

George replied, "Is that a yes?"

Linda was enjoying this cat-and-mouse conversation with Owl and responded, "Definitely, a YES!"

With the rain beginning to fall harder upon the pavement, George asked, "Do you feel like walking over to the Sweet Shop for a cherry Coke? Then again, maybe you better get home. Linda, you are getting soaked."

The wonderfully sensitive Linda took hold of Owl's arm, smiled, and rejoined, "Yeah, isn't it great? I love walking in the rain."

Together, George and Linda left the courtyard, taking a left down Main Street, where the Sweet Shop was tucked in next to the Opera House. By the time they entered the Sweet Shop, both were drenched, Linda still holding on to Owl's right arm. Mr. Connors, standing behind the soda fountain, seeing the two saturated companions, called out, "What the hell have you two been doing? It's pouring out there."

Linda smiled quickly at Owl and vociferously answered, "We are practicing our walk-in for the gala."

Lefky, sitting in his accustomed back booth, hearing Linda's declaration, yelled out, "Hey, everyone, give me a hoot for Owl and Linda. The president has found himself a first lady for the gala."

From the typically jammed Sweet Shop's booths after school were applauses and hoots as Lefky ordered room be made in the booth for Linda and Owl. Lefky put his arm around Owl, remarking, "I knew a fine girl would find you, Owl."

Owl, now emboldened and confident to speak up to Lefky because of his newly found love interest, casually inquired of Lefky, "What are your plans for the gala?"

"Owl," said he, "I have my eye on a filly or two, but I have to consider the pros and cons of each."

Seated with Owl and Linda in the booth were the other members of the tribe, Arse and Bando, and all were pressed in to hear who the two girls under consideration might be, but Lefky drew silent. Bando chimed in, "Hey, I didn't tell you guys that Kelly Zocco is going with me to the gala."

Hearing Bando's announcement after Owl's, Arse got all puffed up and proudly announced, "I asked Karen Gathers, and you know what? She said yes to me. How about that? Lefky you better get with it, or you might be the cheese that stands alone."

Linda, who had never said a word to Arthur Lefkowitz before this moment, proposed, "Arthur, I have a suggestion for you. Why don't you ask Carol Saphora? She just dumped Robert Ragsdale last week. Can you believe it? She gave the "brown helmet" to the best-looking guy in the school. She probably hurting for that stupid move. You could charge right in, and she is beautiful."

Lefky, speaking as candidly as ever, responded, "I know she's hot, but I don't do charity cases."

That comment brought laughter from the tribe and the students in the other surrounding booths.

Just then, Mr. Connors called out, "Lefky, would you please give me a hand?"

Lefky, seated in the middle of the half-circle booth, told all sitting in the booth, "Hey, everybody, get small. I need to get out."

By the front door, Mr. Connors was dragging a mop back and forth, soaking up the water carried in by all the kids coming in from the rain. Mr. Connors asked, "Lefky, would you please hold the door open so I can mop this mess up? I don't want anyone to take a header, coming in or leaving the shop."

Lefky was happy to comply and held the heavy front door of the Sweet Shop wide open so Mr. Connors could mop up the rainwater.

A young lady holding a Pierre Cardin designer umbrella tried to navigate through the open door with the sound of heavy rain hitting Main Street outside of the Sweet Shop.

She was dressed in a long-sleeved orange silk mini dress with ruffled detailing down the front and sleeves, with black patterned hosiery and black and orange pumps; it was none other than she who was regarded as the best-dressed girl in the high school, Joey Galacious.

The epitome of style, Joey attempted to navigate her open umbrella through the door in the heavy rain, only to be deterred as the umbrella's spokes got caught on the door frame. Upon reaching the lip of the doorway, her left three-inch high heel caught in the welcome mat as Joey tripped and fell face down at the Sweet Shop entrance.

Joey let out an "Oh no" as she was sprawled out on the wet surface in front of Mr. Connors and Lefky. Lefky knelt to help Joey up as Joey asked, "Lefky, may I have your arm?"

Joey grabbed Lefky's left arm with both hands and slowly got up, noticing that she had ripped a large run in her nylon hosiery. The consummate fashion diva of the school, a disheveled Joey Galacious, rose in embarrassment as kids sitting in nearby booths raised their eyebrows, covered their mouths in giggles, and stared.

"Lefky, good thing you were here to give me your arm, or I might still be on the floor. Thank you, Lefky," spoke an appreciative Joey.

In a moment of sheer spontaneity, as Joey and Lefky stood before the closed front door of the Sweet Shop, Lefky asked, "Joey, would you be interested in taking my arm one more time? I would like to be your escort at the First Lighting of the Lantern Gala."

Joey was taken aback by this most odd date request. She had dated more than a few boys but never had a guy ask her when she looked like a drowned rat with runs in her nylons. Looking up at the taller Lefky, she began to wonder what her rather buttoned-up mother might say as Lefky interrupted her thoughts. "Joey, I know what people think of me. I know they expect me to horse around and be a jerk, but I promise you, I will treat you with respect every minute of the gala. I promise I will be the perfect gentleman to you."

Joey looked at Lefky and wanted to believe his words were sincere. Smiling, it occurred to her that they would be a center of attention at the gala. She thought, *And what could be wrong with that?*

With that thought, Joey placed her hands on her hips, took a deep breath, and responded, "All right, Mr. Arthur Lefkowitz, I shall accept your invitation to the gala, but mind you, Mr. Lefkowitz, I am holding you to your promise."

Lefky boldly kissed Joey on the lips and announced to one and all, "I just want everyone to know that the beautiful Ms. Joey Galacious has consented to let me be her escort at the gala."

A thunderous cheer arose from the crowd crammed in the booths and at the soda bar. The coupling, the dating requests, and the responses were all but over. It was time for each twosome to select the formal attire in style and color that would adorn them as they proceeded to the receiving line and onto courtyard. Let the gala begin.

Chapter 39

The Gala Cabinet

With the election of junior class officers in hand, the detailed planning for the annual First Lighting of the Lantern Gala began in earnest. Twenty-two of the community's most prestigious local leaders, representing civic and trade groups, industrialists, retailers, and the descendants of many historic families joined together with the new junior class officers to form the gala cabinet, the work group whose mission was to plan and implement the annual First Lighting of the Lantern Gala.

The cabinet embodied a spirit of shared vision with all members, embracing the finest previous renditions of the gala, seeking only to make this year's gala a special memory for all citizens with no personal agenda or desire for self-aggrandizement.

Within the cabinet, separate committees were established to provide detailed procedures and designs for the implementation of courtyard preparation, courtyard flowers, carriages, receiving line protocols, finance, First Kiss Dance Card, junior class officer attire, musical performance, repertoire, princess coronation, photography, nouvelle cuisine and refreshment, and formal *lighting* of the Lantern.

The high school print shop would print and assemble the First Kiss Dance Card, one of the most time-honored features of the gala.

A majestic traditional event, the gala is a formal-attire to marginally formal-attire event. The elegance of the affair dictates that couples of all ages be garmented in their finery, and citizens and students alike look forward to donning exquisite gowns, tuxedos, and the most sophisticated of accessorial elements of formal attire. As one scribe wrote in the local newspaper, "The First Lighting of the Lantern Gala is a time when the local elite come to jingle their jewelry and look to be noticed."

So fine-tuned is the coordination and trust within the gala cabinet that rarely, if ever, do any committee members invade the responsibilities of other members. After the initial meetings of the cabinet, specific lines of communication are drawn and strictly followed until the first horse-drawn carriage arrives at the courtyard on gala evening.

The junior class officers coordinated the school-related aspects of the gala, including erecting two portable stages on the west and south ends of the courtyard, tastefully decorated with sprays of flowers donated by the Greco family. The west stage is used to feature the world-renowned Balahandra String Quartet that would provide music for the receiving line and the early evening traditional dances, waltz and foxtrot, of the gala.

Music of the Gala

The much more extensive south stage is designed to hold the Ricardo Sansouceau Orchestra, an eighteen-piece ensemble with two trios, one female and one male, positioned on either side of the orchestra. The musicians are in formal black, while the female singers are attired in identical sleek floor-length gowns. The male trio will change their dinner jackets throughout the performance, depending on the style of music they perform. One of the marvelous features of the gala is the wide variety of music provided by Ricardo and his orchestra, everything from swing numbers of the 1940s to Motown classics. The effervescent Ricardo, wielding his long white baton, announces every dance by number, alerting the gentlemen in attendance of the dance promised them by a female guest, recorded on each lady's First Kiss Dance Card.

Stephen W. Hoag, Ph.D.

The Gala's Nouvelle Cuisine

One of the exciting features of the First Lighting of the Lantern Gala, as designed by the original cabinet, was the decisions made regarding the role of food. As conceived by the first cabinet, the gala was a celebration of the town of Wallingford, and as with most festivals with a focus on community, it is open to all citizens and must be financially accessible to all. The gala was the coalescence of two significant annual occurrences in town: one was the end of the apple harvest season, and the other was the start of a new high school basketball season.

If the gala had been designed as a large dinner/banquet event, this festival of sorts would immediately be cost-prohibitive for most townspeople, significantly limiting participation. Heretofore, the gala has always been designed as a formal ball, consisting of broad-based traditional music to engender dancing. An endless variety of food with elegant service was planned to enhance the proper atmosphere and the shared experience of dance. Seven flights of carefully prepared nouvelle cuisine finger food are scheduled throughout the gala, with a new flight of at least two new items served by white-jacketed servers every thirty minutes.

Originally a form of French cuisine, nouvelle uses little flour or fat and stresses light sauces and the utilization of fresh seasonal produce that emphasizes lightness and freshness in preparation. The first chef to design the gala's menu was Wallingford resident Jean-Paul Beaufoy, who once served as a pastry chef for one of the robber barons in the Hamptons. The Beaufoy influence is still felt as he enjoyed an eclectic variety of items for each flight.

For this year's gala, three chefs combined their culinary skills to create a new and exciting menu of finger food items for every flight, laying out the finger food flights on round silver trays behind curtained preparation tables.

The flight items included but were not limited to puff pastry, lettuce wraps, *formage*, canapes, bruschetta, crudites, fruit kebabs, mini satay beef skewers, crab cake, shrimp remoulade, olive tapenade, and mushrooms. The chefs and their assistants crafted each item with an emphasis on presentation.

The cabinet and the nouvelle cuisine committee were adamant that the gala would not have the appearance of a buffet. All food is served on silver trays by two white-gloved, white-jacketed servers, working in tandem, offering small six-inch handled plates for ease of handling on which to carry one's food about the courtyard with either white or black linen napkins, contingent upon the dominant color of a guest's formal attire.

Chapter 40

The First Kiss Dance Card

Of the most traditional components of the gala is the First Kiss Dance Card. It has been a tradition since the formal balls of Wallingford, England, centuries ago. The dance card or programme du bal is used by a girl to record the names of the men with whom she intends to dance each dance at a formal ball. Once made of colored scrimshaw, this beautiful item was employed by aristocratic ladies of the Victorian era attending formal events.

For the annual First Lighting of the Lantern Gala, each girl and woman planning to attend the event purchases a First Kiss Dance Card for $3 at the junior class committee booth, set up to sell this cherished article, beginning three weeks before the gala.

On the face of each First Kiss Dance Card, the name of the girl/woman is inscribed. Once folded, the dance card is designed to fit into the palm of the young lady's hand or inserted into the sleeve or cuff of the woman's gown. Opened, the card has numbered lines, 1–14, where the name of each young man requesting a dance from she who is favored is written. The young lady informs each boy of the number of the dance he will be granted her hand in dance. The orchestra leader will announce the dance number before each piece is played.

The First Kiss Dance Card has an important feature, creative and *functioneel*. Draped around the fold of the dance card is a thin woven tassel with an affixed two-inch pencil, used by the woman to write the names of those who would request her hand in dance, and *he* who would taste her lips under the Lantern.

One unique feature is germane to only the First Kiss Dance Card of the First Lighting of the Lantern Gala. At the top of the First Kiss Dance Card is one unique embossed blank line with the two words, "First Kiss." On that line and only that line is the moniker preamble of the Lantern legend, the name of the boy who has asked the young lady to be "the one" for the girl's first kiss then inscribed by she whose lips desire the touch of the lips of he who will forever be emblazoned upon her heart. Under the lit Lantern, this forever "first kiss" is blessed, and as the legend of the Lantern has foretold, "If first kissed under the lantern, your heart shall be moonlit forever after."

Since the first use of the dance card for the gala decades ago, many townspeople have framed the annual sentimental document as it connotes a time of romantic memory and a cherished time of their lives.

Chapter 41

A Regal Departure

One of the unique benefits of being a junior class officer is the tradition of having a two-horse-drawn carriage be your transportation, beginning at any location along Main Street to the front of the courtyard for the gala. The four junior class officers selected various points along Main Street as four carriages with a coachman were dispatched to collect them between 5:30 and 5:45 p.m. for the ten-minute carriage ride.

From the town's early days, carriages and carriage-makers have been part of the transportation and retail landscape. The Conway family has maintained their barns for these ancient carriages for over 150 years, only taking them out for parades and the First Lighting of the Lantern Gala.

Stored in the Conway family barns are four impeccably cared for barouche-style carriages, each brought to this country from Great Britain. Family members tend to these transportation relics as most would a cherished pet with a delicate hand and an awareness of the impact of time and weather elements on crafted wood, brass, and leather. The two matching-color horses added to the magnificence of the carriage.

The slow twelve-minute horse-drawn carriage ride from anywhere on Main Street that will be closed to traffic during the gala permits citizens to walk along Main and witness the spectacle of these historic carriages and their formally attired passengers.

For Class President George Owelowski and his lady in waiting, Linda Rosens, their carriage was drawn by two black horses. The carriages for the class secretary and treasurer and their escorts featured carriages with chestnut horses.

As for Robert Ragsdale and Julia, their carriage would be pulled by two white French Trotters. Adding to the swath of elegance, each junior class officer's name was painted in gold on a white three-foot wooden side, hung by a brass chain on the side of the carriage in which they rode.

As vice president of the junior class, Robert Ragsdale chose his place of departure by horse-drawn carriage to the gala to be at Julia's home on Main Street. The carriage was scheduled to arrive at the Derigg home at 5:30 p.m.

Chapter 42

Julia's Gown

Julia awoke on the morning of the day of the gala with a bit of a giddy-up in her stomach. As she lay on her bed lazily looking up at the ceiling, she wondered if she would look pretty in her gown for Robert or if people would laugh at her.

Julia had tried it on more than a few times with her mother's assistance as this garment was anything but a simple try-on. Mother and daughter found this gown in the same store where her grandfather, Kyle, had picked out the gown for her grandmother many years ago. Her grandmother, Denise, wanted to see her in this gown as soon as she brought it home, but Julia wanted to surprise her grandmother on gala night. Self-doubt entered her mind, and she wondered whether she might make a fool of herself at the gala.

She and Robert practiced dancing the traditional dances about a week before the gala in the sitting room as her mother, Emma, played a few pieces of Chopin, but that was much different from trying to dance in a floor-length gown. For this practice session, Julia wore the shoes she would wear at the gala, a three-inch heel Manolo Blahnik black satin pump, which was a challenge in and of itself. There were so many first-times connected with the gala that Julia wondered whether she could handle all of them.

As with most mornings, Julia's grandmother would drive over to have tea with her daughter, Emma. On this Saturday morning, Julia intercepted her grandmother as she entered the house. Signing her thoughts, Julia asked her grandmother to dispense with having tea and come to her room to have a discussion.

Julia closed the bedroom door as soon as her grandmother sat by the window. Right away, Julia began to sign her anguish about the gala and her multitude of doubts. "I don't know if I can do this. People will be laughing at me. I will embarrass Robert, Mom, Dad and you."

The introspective Denise calmly asked, "What's really bothering you, little one?"

Julia signed back, "Grandmother, I will look stupid. I've never worn a gown of any kind. I've never worn high heels. What if I trip while dancing with Robert? This is a nightmare."

Denise sat next to her cherished granddaughter and spoke softly, "Julia, dear, every girl becomes a woman in her own time. We all have our first time for everything … to dress up … to be in love … to kiss … and to dance." Denise continued with a personal anecdote, "Many years ago, your grandfather made a big deal about our first dance together. He brought me the most lavish formal gown and all the accessories to go along with the gown. I thought this was silly, a formal gown of this elegance to have the first dance with him, but that is your grandfather, always finding his own ways to love."

Julia signed, "What does that mean, finding your ways to love?"

Denise responded, "We'll talk about that in the future, but let me just say this, each of us has to find our special ways to love another person. There is no one size fits all. Your grandfather never stops finding new ways to love me. That is what makes him special." The grandmother continued, "Now how can we get you to calm down and enjoy the gala?"

Julia said, "How can I bring my pad and pen and write notes all night? Everyone will notice and laugh at the mute girl. How can I talk with Robert at the gala without my pad? I can't keep reaching into that little evening bag Mom bought me for my pad and pen."

Denise hugged her granddaughter and suggested, "Leave the pad and pen at home. Talk to Robert with your eyes, like GaaGoo (her dog) talks to you.

I have a feeling he will understand everything you want to say to him. By the way ... lest we forget ... you will have your First Kiss Dance Card with the little pencil attached if you feel the need to write something ... small."

Julia looked across the room at her gala gown hanging in the open walk-in closet across the room. "Grandmother, would you like me to put the gown on for you now?"

Denise retorted, "NO! I'll see it when it wraps itself around you ... tonight."

"So what will *you* be wearing to the gala, Grandmother?" inquired Julia.

Smiling broadly, Denise answered, "Child, I plan to wear something that still gives me quivers and chills."

As it was nearing midafternoon by now, Denise bid her granddaughter goodbye, suggesting, "Let your mother help you with your makeup. Your mother will understand that a little extra zing in your eye shadow always rings a man's heartstrings."

"Anything you say, Grandmother. Will you see me before the carriage arrives to pick me up?"

"Denise replied, "Indeed, I will. I can't wait."

Chapter 43

Time to Assemble
The Ensemble

For an event as significant as the First Lighting of the Lantern Gala, time crawled along for Julia. With their horse-drawn carriage scheduled to arrive at 5:30 p.m., Julia began the step-by-step progression of preparing herself. Making things a little more chaotic at the Derigg household was that her mother, Emma, and father, Scott, would also don their formal regalia, so everybody would be taking extra time to dress and look extra special.

Julia entered her bathroom to prepare her body at 4:00 p.m. as her mother had scheduled her hairdresser to arrive at the Derigg home at 4:30 p.m. to coiffure her thick over-the-shoulder tresses.

Emma also planned to avail herself of the hairdresser with her middle-length hair with bangs.

After completing her makeup and hair with just a touchup of her nails by 5:00 p.m., Julia began the careful step into her magnificent black gown with her mother's assistance.

The formal black gown was of silk with an attached tantalizing flowing organza cape. The dress was designed with a column silhouette and square neckline, showcasing the natural perfection of Julia's petite body. Although sleeveless, the cape element makes for a brilliant accent to her arms.

Floor-length with a left-leg slit, this fully lined silk gown should flow gracefully with her every movement on the courtyard and make dancing with her a dream come true for her escort Robert.

Stepping into her Manolo Blahnik black silk pumps, her shoes are a three-inch covered heel, accented by a crystal buckle at vamp.

With her mother's advice, Julia opted to wear no jewelry on this night with this gown as almost any accessory would only detract from the formal elegance of her raiment. Upon seeing her beautiful daughter adorned by this incredible gown with her hair falling on the sheer fabric covering her shoulders and back, Emma remarked, "Neither the blue diamond of the Nile nor the grand emerald could make you look any more stunning than you do at this moment."

Chapter 44

Julia and Denise
... To Be Awed

The clock ticked to mere minutes before the carriage arrived at the Deriggs' Main Street home to transport Julia and Robert to the gala.

The tall handsome Robert arrived shortly after 5:15 p.m. Julia looked out her bedroom window to view the most attractive thing she had ever seen, Robert. She dared not answer the door. It just wouldn't be right, so her father, Scott, welcomed him.

Mr. Derigg shook Robert's hand and complimented him on his attire. "Robert, my father-in-law would love the tuxedo you are wearing. Tell me about it."

Robert explained, "*My* father picked this tuxedo out for me at a haberdashery he frequents in New York City. It is a Kincaid design with slimmer cut trousers and a lower rise. Father told me the lower rise would be beneficial when dancing."

Mr. Derigg inquired, "What is this fabric? It looks and feels different."

At that very moment, Grandparents Kyle and Denise came through the door, whereupon Kyle spoke out, "My dear Scottie, you should know that this tuxedo is black wool mohair. Your father has good taste, Robert, and you must have impeccable taste yourself, escorting my granddaughter to the gala."

Emma stepped into the foyer and saw her mother, Denise, and declared to her and all who stood in the foyer, "Mother, you did it. You wore the gown. You wore the gown that daddy bought for your first dance all those years ago."

Denise proudly asserted, "Yes, Em, I wanted your father to see me in it one more time. Your father and I shared our first dance over forty years ago in a private box at the Philadelphia Opera House to the strains of 'Bolero.'" Denise continued, "You see, it still fits, and I shall dance with my Kyle throughout the evening."

Kyle remembered and joyfully described the gown he personally selected all those years ago and his magnificent Denise wore on this night. "Look at my Denise," Kyle beckoned all, "in her liquid black column gown with soft pleating in front, and oh, that halter neckline that ties at the nape of her neck, that sensitive place I have placed gentle kisses.

"Of course, the feature of this dress that always drove me wild is the thigh-high slit, and I can see that my beloved has not lost her fastball."

Emma declaratively added, "Daddy, if you like your wife's gown, you better fasten your seat belt and ensure that your seat backs and tray tables are in their upright positions as you are about to take the first view of your granddaughter, Julia."

At that moment, the horse-drawn carriage pulled up to the stone walkway of their house. Kyle, Denise, Scott, and Emma stood in the large open front door looking at the majestic white carriage led by two white horses and a nattily dressed coachman.

As for Robert, his eyes lifted to the long staircase that led to the foyer where the resplendent Julia stood at the top of the landing.

Julia, with a smile meant for Robert, slowly descended the steps. Robert took a few steps up on the staircase to guide her down the winding stairs, but Julia motioned to him to let her walk the stairs alone with her left hand sliding along the banister.

As Julia reached the bottom of the staircase, Robert offered his right arm, and she placed her left hand on his arm.

Robert whispered, "You are the most beautiful girl in the world. My Julia, your carriage awaits."

Together, they strode through the open front door where her parents and grandparents turned in glowing awe of their Julia and her beau.

Chapter 45

The Magic of "Getting There"

Julia and Robert walked the cobblestone walkway from the front door of the Derigg house to the right side of the carriage as the coachman attached a three-stair step stool to the side of the carriage.

With parents, Emma and Scott, and grandparents, Denise and Kyle, lining the walkway, all their eyes were on the radiant Julia. Within an hour, all would be at the gala with elegantly dressed everyone flooding all eyes on the courtyard pageantry.

The coachman stood ready by the step stool to assist Julia into the carriage but deferred to Robert, who was attending her every step. Reaching to grasp the long cape so it would escape surface dirt or cause Julia to misstep, Julia took the three steps of the stool into the leather bench seat of the carriage. Sliding to the left on the bench seat, Julia was careful not to sit on any part of her gown that wasn't necessary, so she draped her cape across the front of her. Robert stepped into the carriage and sat close to her right. He was inclined to wrap his arm around her but was content to place his left hand on her right hand, making them both smile.

The coachman detached the stairs and placed them in the boot of the carriage. Taking his place at the front of the carriage, he took the reins of the two horses in his hands and looking over his right shoulder, asked, "May I drive you to the gala?"

Savoring the rhetorical question, Robert replied, "Drive on, sir, and please take your time."

The setting sun that seemed to summon a starburst of color on the horizon was a perfect backdrop for their carriage ride down Main Street to the First Lighting of the Lantern Gala. With no automobiles on the road, all of Main Street was a driveway to the gala. Passing the historic homes, Julia thought of all the times she had walked her GaaGoo, and never once did she ever feel so alive inside and out, never had she felt so pretty.

Robert's thoughts were all about Julia, and he kept turning his eyes to her, drinking in every feature, from her glistening hair to her hazel eyes.

Julia's heart too was filled with Robert, and in the slow carriage ride to the gala, listening to the hoof beats of the white horses on the pavement, Julia turned to Robert and signed. Her thumb and index finger formed an L with her pinky lifted as her middle and ring finger curled and touched her palm. Julia pointed that gesture at Robert.

Looking at her quizzically, Robert asked, "So what does that mean?"

Julia shook her head, indicating, "No."

"You mean you aren't going to tell me?" pressed Robert.

Once again, Julia slowly shook her head no.

With no pad to write on, for the present, no meant no.

Passing the Sweet Shop on their right, many people were already lined up on Main Street in their finery, waiting for the Burgher to open the gala at the receiving line at 6:30 p.m.

As their carriage arrived at the east end of the courtyard, their eyes were filled with the most lavish decorations of flowers and cascading bolts of satin and other fabrics arranged to billow like long blue and gold vertical clouds all around the courtyard.

The south stage where the Ricardo orchestra will perform and the coronation ceremony will take place was trimmed in purple blue roses (Zennixplus) donated by the Wykeham Nurseries that grow these rare roses specifically for the annual gala. The smaller west stage, already active with the string quartet tuning their instruments, is decked out in an assortment of white and red flowers.

Soon after 6:00 p.m., the carriage carrying Robert and Julia arrived at the Main Street entrance to the gala as the other horse-drawn carriages carrying the other junior class officers had pulled up to the curb.

A dramatic twenty-foot canopy of white draped sheer voile in a crisscross pattern served as the entranceway that began at the sidewalk and was the perfect precursor to the receiving line and the elegant courtyard.

Julia stepped down from her carriage with Robert holding her cape's flowing waves and left arm. They paused at the beginning of the canopy, looking at each other as Robert whispered, "Julia, everything will be perfect. By the way, may I have the first dance on your dance card?"

Walking under the canopy, they were met by the Burgher responsible for the receiving line.

Let the gala begin.

Chapter 46

The Receiving Line, The Burgher, and The General

Since the First Lighting of the Lantern Gala, the formality of the occasion, from top to bottom, made the gala the finest local event of any type each year. One of the components that make the gala so indescribable and desirable for every citizen to attend is the manner in which everyone is welcomed to the gala. If you are a citizen of the town, dressed in formal attire or garments clearly illustrating your commitment to wearing your finery to the gala, you are granted admittance with no monetary charge. Age, profession, or walk of life does not matter as long as you are dressed according to protocol and speak "the Burgher's request."

People begin assembling for the gala around 6:00 p.m. along Main Street. This allows townspeople to see the gowns and finery of each person standing in line as they wait to walk the receiving line before the gala's official start at 7:00 p.m.

At 6:15 p.m., with five dramatic thrusts of the Burgher's staff on the courtyard surface, the string quartet on the west stage of the courtyard played the welcome opening piece, Boccherini's String Quartet in E Major, Opus 11-5, Minuet, to be followed by Beethoven's No. 15 in A Minor, Opus 132; Shostakovich's String Quartet No. 8 in C Minor, Opus 110; and Franz Shubert's String Quartet, No. 14 in D. Minor.

Each person attending the gala is considered a "guest" and treated as such as everyone in the community is cordially invited. Indeed, there are some gate crashers from other communities, but they are few and far between.

The only requirement for a couple's entry to the gala is that the gentleman of the couple must utter the time-honored words spoken to the Burgher, known as "The Burgher's Request":

> "We, (names of the couple), do hereby request the courtesy of the evening to be welcomed to the First Lighting of the Lantern Gala."

This verbal protocol for admittance for every guest, reaching back over a century, is spoken to the Wallingford Burgher, the maitre d' of the gala, who stands at the entranceway to the receiving line, the required passageway onto the courtyard. The Burgher is always dressed in a black morning suit, tuxedo with tails, with striped slacks.

After stating their intentions to the Burgher, who holds a three-foot ornate staff with a brass ferrule, the Burgher strikes the pavement twice with his staff, signaling to the couple that they may proceed down the line of receiving. This entrance protocol to the gala has been unchanged for decades, and the position of the Burgher is one of honor and sophistication.

As each dignitary included in the receiving line arrives, the Burgher places each of them in order. First in the receiving line is the Honorable President of the Gala Cabinet, Dr. Abbott J. Wachtelhausen; then House of Burgesses members, Millard Williamson and Dr. Bartholonew Sagraves; followed by Mr. William McCain, high school principal, and Mrs. Hildagaard Loomis, teacher and town historian. The final eight members of the receiving line were Junior Class President George Owelowski, his lady fair, Linda Rosens; Junior Class Vice President Robert Ragsdale and Julia Derigg, Junior Class Secretary Kathy Reynolds and her escort, John Ranzino; Junior Class Treasurer, Paula Anderson, and her escort, Francis Parfait.

At the end of the thirteen-person receiving line stands the stately retired general of the army, Marcus Linton, a distinguished gentleman, and a United States Military Academy graduate. Each year General Linton wears his formal uniform to the gala, adorned with all the medals he has been awarded in thirty years in the service of our country. On his left hip hung an army saber encased in a scabbard that he only wears in parades and the annual gala.

A member of the gala cabinet, the general assumes one responsibility for the gala: He coordinates the selection process and coronation of the gala queen.

As each couple proceeds along the receiving line, sharing words of welcome and expectations for an evening of wonderment, compliments flow in recognizing the beauty of every gown and the radiance of every face.

General Linton, the last person to offer a greeting at the line's end, has one special duty to perform. With each person who completes the walk along the receiving line, the general presents them with a silk-finished 3.5-inch card. On the front of the card are the words "First Lighting of the Lantern Gala Queen." The broad-voiced general enthusiastically instructs each guest to write the name of the woman/girl the guest selects as the gala queen on the back of the card and that all cards are to be returned to him no later than 8:00 p.m. The general points to the large navy blue velvet sack he carries on his right shoulder, where the ballots are to be deposited and readied for the counting process. General Linton concludes his directions with, "All must vote. Be not last, or I shall note the absence of your vote."

The "demanding" order from the general himself makes everyone smile and want to comply.

The first guests to walk the receiving line was Arthur "Lefky" Lefkowitz, escorting Joey Galacious, who wore a sleeveless blue sequin tulle mermaid-style form-fitting gown with a strapless sweetheart neckline. Lefky, a good-sized young man, size 46, wore a black double-breasted tuxedo with peak lapels and a double-vent jacket. Upon approaching the Burgher, Lefky stated the required request, "We, Arthur Lefkowitz and Josephine Galacious, do hereby request the courtesy of the evening to be welcomed to the First Lighting of the Lantern Gala."

The Burgher bowed gracefully and replied, "Arthur and Josephine, we welcome you," and struck the pavement twice with his three-foot staff.

Lefky and Joey proceeded to walk the receiving line, shaking hands with all thirteen dignitaries. When Lefky got to Arse and Owl in the receiving line, he called them by their proper names. To Arse, he said, "Arsenella, she is too pretty for you, so treat her well this evening." To Owl, he said, "George, I am very proud of you," then turning to Linda Rosens, his date, he said, "He is a good guy, be kind to him."

In the last ten minutes of guests proceeding along the receiving line was Carol Saphora, wearing a gold off-shoulder sparkly sequin sleeveless gown. She held the arm of John Kellin, who had long ago fallen in love with her and swooned at Carol's locker each day since he was in ninth grade. As Carol reached the end of the receiving line where Robert and Julia stood, she looked at Robert, saying clearly for nearby people to hear, "Well, I hope you are very proud of yourself."

John Kellin lightly pulled on Carol's arm, quietly saying for Carol's ears only, "He (Robert) is old news. He'll feel it tonight when you are named gala queen."

As each couple completed the welcoming salutations of the receiving line, some immediately wrapped themselves in a dancing embrace, while others joined with others they knew in the joyful attendees of the gala.

Central in the proceedings of the gala were the constant appearances of the First Kiss Dance Cards by the women in attendance. While most of the female guests bought their First Kiss Dance Cards well in advance of the gala, some opted to buy their First Kiss Dance Card upon arrival before walking down the receiving line.

The first flights of cuisine carried forth by the extensive white-jacketed serving staff circulated through every vestige of the courtyard. Meanwhile, the traditional gala non-alcoholic punch added to the ambience as it was brilliantly served from four silver fountains with surrounding ice carvings. As the courtyard was filled with dancing and little gatherings generating giggles and compliments galore for every lady in attendance, Mr. McCain, while dancing with his wife, noticed Arthur Lefkowitz and his date standing by one of the punch fountains and scurried over to chat with the well-known Lefky.

Quietly but authoritatively, he spoke, "Now, Arthur, this is a punch fountain, carefully prepared by the gala cabinet committee, and I think you would agree that introducing any alcoholic substance into the punch would be an insult to those people who prepared this beverage."

Lefky, responded, rather indignantly, "Now, Mr. McCain, I hope you are not suggesting that I would ever do anything so despicable as spiking the gala punch."

With that assurance, Mr. McCain and his wife returned to their dancing, at which point, Joey Galacious, Lefky's date, whispered to him, "Didn't I hear that you spiked the punch at last year's gala?"

Lefky would only wink at Joey and bid her dance with him.

The First Lighting of the Lantern Gala was in full swing as the string quartet gave way to the sounds of Ricardo Sansouceau Orchestra, whose first song was a request of the junior class officers as a tribute to their special place, the Sweet Shop, "Green Onions."

Chapter 47

Julia's First Kiss
Dance Card

With the receiving line dissolved, Robert took Julia by the hand and led her to the edge of the courtyard dance surface. Julia stubbornly stopped dead in her tracks and reached into her black satin evening bag, slung over her shoulder with a gold chain. Robert thought Julia had her pad and pen inside the bag and maybe wanted to write something to him, but Julia had other things in mind.

She took out a First Kiss Dance Card with its attached mini-pencil. She sternly yet playfully looked at Robert and pointed to her dance card. Owl and Linda were dancing nearby as George, Owl, suggested, "She's not going to dance with you unless you request a dance."

Robert laughed, speaking to her, "Julia, may I have dance no. 2 with you?"

Julia shook her head "no."

"What?" Robert inquired.

Julia opened the dance card and raising it to his face, took the attached pencil and made a big circle around the numbers of the dances 1–10. With the mini-pencil, she wrote across the dance numbers and blank lines, "ALL for Robert."

Robert took Julia's hands in his. "As you wish. I will dance every dance with you. No one else gets to dance with you, except maybe your father or grandfather."

They finally took a break from dancing, accepted plates from the servers with napkins, and had a little to eat, but moments later, when Ricardo called out no. 15, they were back in each other's arms for the song "I Only Have Eyes for You."

The slow dances came very naturally to Julia. Robert made it all seem so easy. He held her right hand high in his left hand, and his right hand was gently placed under her right shoulder blade, so when he turned, Julia turned gracefully with him.

They sat out a few dances, finding two unoccupied chairs near the pole where a hook suspended the coveted Lantern. Later in the evening, after the coronation, the gala queen would light the Lantern.

The Blank First Line

As Julia and Robert sat with plates of finger food, Julia placed her plate on the surface below her and signed the same gesture she had during the carriage ride to the gala. Julia's thumb and index finger formed an L with her pinky finger lifted as her middle and ring finger curled and touched her palm. Julia pointed that gesture at Robert and then crossed her arms in front of her.

Robert looked carefully into her eyes and asked again, "What does that mean?"

If there was a moment in her life she longed to speak, this was it. She pursed her lips, then parted them, clearly showing Robert that she wanted to speak words to him. Finally, showing the frustration she had known all her life, she reached for her First Kiss Dance Card with the little attached pencil.

Robert encouraged her, "Julia, write down what you want to say like you always do on your pad."

Julia looked at him and was just about to write something on her First Kiss Dance Card when General Linton's booming voice came over the microphone, announcing that all ballots for the gala queen had to be in his hands *now*.

163

Neither Robert nor Julia had completed their gala queen ballot, so they scurried to find them, Robert in his inside pocket and Julia in her evening bag.

Robert asked Julia to use her little pencil and wrote on the back of his card the name Julia Derigg. Julia shook her head no, watching Robert write her name, but Robert only smiled and said, "It's my vote, and I vote for you."

Julia held her ballot in her hand, smiled knowingly, and wrote the name of one of the few girls who ever showed her kindness, Diane Deere. Robert crossed the courtyard and placed the two ballots in the general's blue velvet bag.

Before returning to the dance floor, Robert pressed again to learn the meaning of the sign Julia directed at him. Julia opened her dance card and pointed to the embossed first line of the dance card with the imprinted words "First Kiss."

Robert didn't know quite what to say. Without words, Robert pointed to that blank space, touched his lips with his index finger, and then touched Julia's lips. They stared into each other's eyes, Julia wanting but unable to speak and Robert choosing not to speak.

For the next hour, Julia held Robert's arm as they walked around the courtyard, both with so much they wanted to say but choosing to remain silent. Julia thought only of the boy she met in Algebra II class, whom she would have never known except for his math difficulties.

He was so good-looking, but Julia found him to be kind, gentle, and talented. People said he was good at basketball, but she didn't care about basketball.

She had passed him in the hallways many times but never thought she would hold his arm, let alone dance with him at the gala.

Robert never gave this little mute girl a second thought before the embarrassment he felt in Algebra II class. It was as though she was invisible to him. Then suddenly, he saw this beautiful girl before him, and she wanted to help him.

He thought he knew what it felt like to be in love, but now Julia had taught him what love was all about through her inability to speak, using her hands and eyes to speak to him, and giving of herself with kindness, the inner strength of character, her beauty.

Everyone in town said that the gala was always the best time and place to dance because the live music was without equal and nonstop. Julia discovered she loved to dance, and Robert made her feel like the best dancer at the gala, even though this was the first time she had ever danced with a boy.

Robert was still perplexed by the meaning of the signing that Julia had twice directed at him. Standing in the middle of the courtyard with the music playing and people dancing all around them, Julia grabbed Robert's hands to stop dancing for a moment. The noise was palpable, and it didn't matter at all to them. Julia took out her dance card and showed Robert the blank space for "First Kiss." This time Robert pointed at himself and pointed to the blank line at the top of the First Kiss Dance Card. Julia gave him the sign for *yes*. Robert curled his fingers in a fist and nodded with his hand in the sign *yes*. Julia put Robert's hands together like an open book. She laid the dance card on his hands and wrote in the blank embossed space, "Robert Ragsdale."

There was a time for a first kiss. Julia's grandmother, Denise, had told her so just this morning, but the first kiss would come in its own time.

Julia and Robert returned to the dancing of the gala and the feeling of holding each other. The night was still young, and a first kiss was promised, but when?

Chapter 48

The Coronation

By 7:30 p.m., with the full moon hovering overhead against the backdrop of a deep blue sky, the courtyard was full of dancing couples in the cool breeze of the evening. Some chose to dance in a continuous embrace with a woman's arms about her gentleman escort's neck. Others demanded additional space on the courtyard, preferring to dance apart from their partner, partaking in spins and twirls. No matter the variation of dance or the many types of music provided by the string quartet and the orchestra that swirled about everyone, one could still faintly hear the rustle of flowing gowns and the clatter of high-heel shoes upon the courtyard surface. General Linton circulated the multitude, constantly reminding everyone to place their completed vote card in the large velvet sack that hung on his shoulder if they hadn't already done so.

The general's velvet sack was growing heavy, burgeoning with completed card ballots. It was a traditional part of the gala that everyone took most seriously, to choose the gala queen. The nature of the process allowed no time should some selfish individual wish to lobby for this recognition, so people danced, imbibed the non-alcoholic gala punch, ate, circulated, and most importantly, observed the many exquisitely attired females in attendance, anyone a candidate to be the gala queen. The final selection was always a surprise to everyone as there were always well over two hundred women in attendance. In some few feet of the courtyard, danced or elegantly sat an unsuspecting girl/woman who would be proclaimed gala queen at 10:00 p.m., and her coronation would ensue.

At precisely 8:00 p.m., the general and two of his subordinates, Esther Earley and Charles Tyrrell, retired to the black curtained vestry behind the food preparation tables. With expertise in having performed the task of counting the silken vote cards in previous galas, the general, Mrs. Earley, and Mr. Tyrrell began separating the vote cards alphabetically.

From Angelone to Zabora, named ballots were laid out on three eight-foot tables, away from wandering eyes and nosy minds. Methodically, stacks emerged as some names were written on ballots repeatedly. It became clear to the three ballot counters that seven to ten different women were the most popular vote-getters, making them strong candidates for gala queen.

With so many women of all ages in attendance, from Abigail Beach, age ninety-four, to little Regina Saty, age eight, daughter of John and Sherry Saty, there were a seemingly endless number of persons receiving balloted attention at the gala.

Sifting through the names on the silken gala queen cards was a tedious and time-consuming process, but under the leadership of General Linton and his two assistants, rapid progress was made.

Shortly after 9:00 p.m., all voting cards had been alphabetically aligned, and a few names garnered repeated attention on the scores of ballots. Four stacks of cards distinguished themselves from all the rest.

General Linton summoned his two assistants and instructed them to count the cards in each stack one more time carefully. Mrs. Earley and Mr. Tyrrell agreed on their count, leaving one name clearly atop the others.

The general rose from his chair, saying the name of the gala queen for the first time, and asked if either knew the girl. Mrs. Earley acknowledged that the queen-elect was a junior at the high school and that she lived on Main Street. The general asked Mr. Tyrrell to please check the guest list and see if the parents of the queen-elect might be in attendance. Scanning the sign-in guest list, Tyrrell discovered that not only were the queen-elect's parents on the courtyard but so were her grandparents too. General Linton was most pleased as he now could include them all in the coronation ceremony.

At 9:45 p.m., General Linton ordered the cessation of all food flights until after the coronation as the white-jacketed servers assumed a new role. Parting the dancing guests on the courtyard like Moses parted the Red Sea, the servers unfurled an eight-foot-wide by a twenty-foot-long white runner with gold trim down the middle of the courtyard, ending at the west stage of the courtyard. Simultaneously, four servers carried the traditional gala queen throne to center stage in front of the orchestra.

With its stunning curves and classic Italian baroque design, this wingback chair, created atop a sturdy mahogany frame with scrolled arms and an exaggerated high back, is upholstered in white velvet hand-finished in a rich gold leaf. Indeed, this throne was befitting of the gala queen.

General Linton dispatched Mrs. Earley to locate the parents and grandparents of the queen-elect, making sure not to tip off the family or the girl about to be announced as queen. Mrs. Earley approached the grandparents. The general asked Mrs. Earley to promote a ruse per se. If the grandparents or parents pressed for a reason for the request to meet with the general, Mrs. Earley was to suggest that something had been found that might belong to them. Obviously, the general had employed this little lie before.

Mrs. Earley found the grandparents, Kyle and Denise, on the courtyard, dancing to a marvelous rendition of the 1970s song "It Keeps You Running," as Mrs. Earley insisted that they immediately follow her to meet with General Linton.

Denise and Kyle's daughter, Emma, and her husband Scott, also dancing, spotted them leaving the courtyard with Mrs. Earley and thought there might be a problem brewing and promptly followed them to the curtained area behind the chefs' food preparation tables.

The general invited the parents and grandparents to be seated, at which point the good general first asked, "Did your daughter, granddaughter know you were coming back here to meet with me?"

Julia's mother, Emma, observed, "General, my daughter is hopelessly enthralled in the haze of infatuation of her escort. I doubt she would acknowledge the arrival of Santa Claus in his sleigh."

Grandmother Denise glibly corrected her daughter, "General Linton, she passed infatuation on the giddy-meter days ago. The child is certainly *in love.*"

General Linton interrupted this stream of lightheartedness and stated, "You (parents and grandparents) are, henceforth, sworn to secrecy for the next thirty minutes. Do I have your word?"

Denise responded immediately, "About what, General?"

"I have the distinct privilege to inform you that your daughter," pointing to Emma and Scott, "and your granddaughter," pointing to Denise and Kyle, "has been named gala queen."

Immediately, Grandmother Denise chirped, "Sweet Jesus."

As the parents and grandparents hugged each other, the general began to explain, "I asked you to meet with me in seclusion because I want to request that you be part of the coronation."

All agreed to assist in any way they could. The general told them to stay close to the west stage for the announcement at 10:00 p.m.

Pronouncement

Orchestra maestro, Ricardo, taking a cue from General Linton at 9:50 p.m., stepped to the microphone. "Honored guests, ladies and gentlemen, it gives the Sansouceau Orchestra the greatest pleasure to introduce world-renown trumpeter Estaban Cologne to present the queen's flourishes."

Ricardo raised his baton as the orchestra played the introduction of the "La Virgen de la Macarena." The assembled guests on the gala courtyard all knew the music and what great moment would follow. With his brass trumpet flashing in the evening lights, Cologne primed the crowd with a brilliant performance of the gala queen's introductory music.

As the soloist performed a dazzling outro, signaling the conclusion of the gala queen's music, General Linton climbed the five steps of the west stage to stand behind the microphone just to the left of the white and gold queen's throne.

The general needed to do little to quell the noise of the hundreds of guests before him as a hush fell over the courtyard. Every eye was trained on the general as everyone knew of the general's mission at 10:00 p.m.

At precisely 10:00 p.m., the gala's guests packed tightly along the sides of the white runner with gold trim. General Linton stepped to the microphone, authoritatively explaining, "I am about to introduce to you the name of your gala queen. Whomever she may be, I am requesting that her attendant lead her to the east end of the queen's runway, walk the runway, escorting her onto the stage for the coronation."

The silence was profound on the gala courtyard as General Linton spoke the words of his deep reverence to the town he loved. "Honored guests, fellow citizens of our fair town, ladies and gentlemen, I have walked along the cobblestones and pavement of Main Street since I was a boy. I have passed you on that sidewalk as we have hurried along to school, church, a workplace, a shop, or just the peaceful act of walking on familiar ground where we share the common threads of community collegiality.

"For me, there is no more incredible honor than announcing our gala queen's name. This year, as in all years, I embrace your many reasons for selecting this queen as she represents the best of our town. I have never met her and know nothing of her, but I know, without equivocation, that if you, my fellow Wallingford citizens, have selected her, there is no finer person, no more beautiful woman in any town in the world."

Taking a deep breath and expanding his barrel chest, General Linton bellowed, "Honored guests, indeed, ladies and gentlemen, I present to you for the first time, your gala queen *Julia Derigg*."

From held-breath anticipation, a deafening hail enveloped the gala guests. Even the many guests who did not know Julia shouted, "The queen!" and thundered applause.

In his black tuxedo, Robert looked deeply into Julia's tear-filled eyes after the initial moments of the announcement were made by the general, who spoke softly to Julia, "It's OK to cry, Julia. It's OK."

The diminutive beauty looked at him in tight-lipped frustration. Her heart was filled with an excitement she could have never imagined, and she could not express her feelings to Robert as she had determined not to carry her pad with her at the gala. Julia tried to fight back the tears of joy and with no other communication venue available to her, signed to Robert, knowing that Robert could only watch her signing.

Robert watched her hand gestures of signing and stretched his heart out so that he might be able to understand the language of signing. Placing his hands in a cupping pose in front of him, he signed the only word he knew that Julia had taught him, "yes." With both hands, he made a fist and nodded with both. Indeed, this moment of the gala queen was all "yes."

A Moment

General Linton motioned to Julia's parents and grandparents to follow Julia onto the stage. Robert lifted the cape of Julia's gown as she walked the stairs to the high-back white throne. Robert assisted Julia in assuming the throne as Scott and Emma and Kyle and Denise took their places behind the new queen.

The continuous applause and cheering were momentarily quelled by the general, who spoke to the gala crowd. "Ladies and gentlemen, I am honored to place the crown of the gala queen upon her, a magnificent silver tiara decorated with diamonds and sapphires, provided and set in her tiara by the Lakeshire family and their outstanding jewelers, serving our community for seven generations."

General Linton placed the queen's tiara on Julia with the words, "You, *Julia Derigg*, are hereby named queen of the First Lighting of the Lantern Gala with all the rights and privileges bestowed on you. May your reign as queen be forever blessed, and may all your dreams come true.

"My fellow citizens, I present *Queen Julia*."

With that pronouncement, the courtyard was filled with a tumultuous roar.

Chapter 49

The First Lighting of The Lantern

General Linton approached the microphone. "And now, our queen of the gala, as your first official act, it is time for you to light the flame for the First Lighting of the Lantern.

"Mr. Robert Ragsdale, would you please escort our gala queen, Julia Derigg, followed by her parents, Scott and Emma, and grandparents, Kyle and Denise, to the Lantern, where the Burgher will present you with the torch for the 'first lighting.'"

Julia placed her left hand on Robert's arm and rose from her throne. Robert guided her every step down the staircase to once again step onto the white runner positioned in the gala's middle for the short walk to the west corner of the courtyard, where the Lantern hung proudly.

On the white walkway through the middle of the courtyard to the west corner, the ten-foot wooden pole stood erect as it had since 1936, with the metal Lantern suspended at the pole's top with an iron hook.

The town Burgher held a lit six-foot torch in his hands. At the base of the pole was a five-step wooden ladder.

As Queen Julia approached the ladder, the Burgher, Robert, held the longest part of her black gown. Carefully, Julia climbed the five steps with her right on Robert's shoulder. At the top of the five stairs, the Burgher handed Julia the lit torch with these words, "Queen Julia, please light the lantern for all to see."

With both hands, Julia reached up as far as she could with the six-foot torch and ignited the candle in the open Lantern as Robert held her in place. The flicker of the candle became a brilliant multicolor glow in the confines of the metal-filtered Lantern as the 340 persons in attendance applauded wildly.

The lights all around the courtyard and the block of Main Street on which the high school sits were dimmed at the lighting of the Lantern. All guests of the gala were moved by the moment they shared and the promise of the future each envisioned.

Chapter 50

A Forever Moment—
The First Kiss

With the Lantern lit, General Linton approached the microphone at the front of the south stage. The general spoke, "We, as citizens of our fair town, have long celebrated our Lantern and its role in local lore, but we have also revered the legend of the Lantern that I now recite to you, 'If first kissed under the lantern, forever moonlit will be thy heart.'"

The general continued, "May all your kisses be heaven blessed, and may your heart know only the purity of love."

Julia returned the lit torch to the Burgher and stood arm in arm with Robert under the lit Lantern. To one side of them were her parents, Emma and Scott, and to the other, the introspective and sentimental Denise and her husband, Kyle. They gave their daughter/granddaughter space at this moment that she would never forget. Emma's thoughts were of the girl she raised without a voice who had withstood years of social isolation and look at her now.

The gala guests began moving toward the Lantern for their special moments. Julia and Robert were facing each other under the lit Lantern. Julia opened her evening purse that her grandmother was carrying for her during the lighting of the Lantern. She took out the First Kiss Dance Card, opened it, and peered into Robert's joyful eyes. Julia pointed to Robert's name on the first line under the embossed words "First Kiss."

175

Directly under the lit Lantern, Julia and Robert faced each other. Robert lovingly embraced Julia, holding her against him. Taller, he tilted his face down, their chins touching.

Julia wanted this moment as Denise had foretold. With the softness of a raindrop on a rose petal, their eyes closed, lips touched, and lingered in their first kiss, Julia's first kiss.

Julia heard the sound of her heartbeat, feeling a gush of emotion she had never known. As their lips parted, no sign could express her feeling at that moment. In that instant, there was only Robert and her in the world.

With her arms around Robert's neck and Robert's arms enfolded about her, they beheld more than each other. They had become a singular emotion absent a definition, without a next moment. Their first kiss was a forever kiss.

Julia, who had lived in silence all her life, keeping every thought and feeling tucked deep in her soul, felt the swelling of her pounding heart and could not withstand the tidal wave of joy that demanded to be let loose. With her parents and grandparents compelled by all their love to drink in all that was Julia in this trice, they remained motionless.

Julia tried to speak to Robert with her eyes, but it wasn't enough.

Drawing close to his lips again, Julia placed her hands on either side of his face and tilting her head so slightly, parting her lips, dropping her jaw, *spoke* gently, "BOBBEEEE."

Julia had spoken. A lump instantly emerged in the throats of her parents and grandparents. They all looked at each other, and tears flowed from them.

It took a few seconds for Julia to realize what had just happened, what she had said. She spoke a word.

Robert feather-kissed her lips and whispered, "Julia."

Julia kissed him in the same fashion and said with growing confidence, "BOBBEE."

Suddenly aware of the loving family around her, she turned to them and pointed to her mouth, making no further attempts at words.

Denise looked at Julia through tears that would not be quelled and spoke, "Little one, for every woman, there are first times. You have had few this day."

Gala guests were starting to line up for their first kisses under the Lantern as Julia, Robert, and her family members moved to the side with many bidding Julia congratulatory thoughts on her being named gala queen.

Still moved by the events under the Lantern, Grandmother Denise kissed her husband Kyle and asked him, "Do you think Robert is 'the one'?"

Kyle placed his index finger on Denise's lips, outlining them as he had done so many years ago, and said, "There is only one. You are 'the one.' Julia will find her 'one' in good time. Let us celebrate the glory of all that has just happened.

"Our Julia is gala queen. She has just spoken a word. Julia is in love."

Miracles do happen on Main Street.

Epilogue

There is a chemistry in every relationship, a composition of exchanged emotions, shared activities, and the catalytic responsiveness of each individual to another. In the vibrant confines of each high school, a dynamic age of innocence gives way to an epoch of discovery and enlightenment, leading to adulthood. Usually fraught with challenge and tribulation, the high school years are retrospectively viewed as the best years of one's life.

In *Main Street: Anyone's Town, Everyone's Forever*, you have been joyfully welcomed into the lives of a few dozen young men and women. Their stories, however brief and interwoven in this harmonious tale of unrelenting ontogenesis, are but a beginning to the lives they will lead in the days and years to come.

The eternal fire, ignited on the pages of this novel, brilliantly ablaze in the hearts and entwined lives of the players in this ongoing song, will return in the continuing saga of Main Street. To wit, this story is a song that has more verses to be sung to you.

Acknowledgments

The years of writing *Main Street: Anyone's Town, Everyone's Forever* is the confluence of a lifetime of observations, influences, and learning moments. To the many incredible people I have admired, may these pages do justice to the remarkable beauty, notable personalities, and the romantic haze they combined to create in my thoughts.

My endless appreciation to friend, "handler," the whirlwind, Jill DeChello (and her "tribe"), who work tirelessly and with extraordinary enthusiasm on my behalf to create the grandest of events.

With gratitude for the myriad of kindnesses given to me during a long and momentous lifetime and career, I must acknowledge A. Todd Sagraves, John Barberino, Thomas Welch, Patrick Saty, Terry Pendleton, John Hrehowsik, Tarn Granucci, and Barry O'Brien. I'd like to express my thanks to Maureen DiSorbo who conducted such a detailed edit of this book.

The number of people who unknowingly touched this piece is endless. To all the Wallingford citizenry, students, teachers, coaches, and family who supported and encouraged the research necessary to complete this writing, from concept to the fullest manifestation of its intended purpose, you have my endless appreciation.

Special thanks to the tremendously talented Tony Falcone for creating the amazing cover image, David Frost for the photography, and the forever inspiration, "The One," the magnificent Denise.

Main Street, ...the Poem

This poem was written in 1974 by Stephen W. Hoag, then a young teacher seeking his heart's desire while leaning on the memories of the street he cherished in his early life.

Less a stroll, more a daily tour,
> a walk down Main Street, a memory brochure.

The sidewalk once a boundary of grass and stone,
> Main Street, a road of ancient homes and tales unknown.

Autos motor down Main where once horse and carriage did tread,
> still, the giant elms line the byway with a sparkling of flower beds.

Every road has a narrative that whistles in the din,
but Main Street possesses a legacy of moments that sing in the wind.

The bells of the churches on Main each Sunday will chime
> as worshippers of each faith climb the stairs seeking the divine.

Of the moments on Main, there were marching bands and parades,
> celebrating great victories and decorated brigades.

From the first and forever Main Street is the people who walked,
> the smiles that were shared, often the tears, the banters, and talk.

Sauntering along the pavement, heading for the movies or a game,
holding hands, stealing kisses, building passion and flame.

People glanced from their windows to see the pretty girls striding by,
and the occasional athletic boy in jacket and tie.

Springtime on Main Street brought the evening with cars of
tall pointed fins,
and girls in convertibles and with their tresses in the wind.

Someday, if there is a girl for me, I know I will walk with her
on Main.
We'll fall in love as lovers do, and I'll kiss her in the rain.

Author Page

An innovative, passionate educator, football coach, and mentor, Dr. Hoag was a Connecticut State Department of Education member for over thirty-five years. An accomplished speaker, he has entertained and thrilled audiences throughout his lifetime with his anecdotes and philosophy on teaching, parenthood, athletic coaching, and student leadership.

Dr. Hoag has received state and national recognition for teaching, coaching, education assessment, and community service. Of the many awards, Dr. Hoag was the recipient of the national 2008 C. Thomas Olivio Award, presented to one person annually for leadership and creativity in student assessment by the National Occupational Competency Testing Institute. In 2013, Dr. Hoag was honored with the Silver Eagle Award of the Connecticut Council of Deliberation for "sterling service to uplift humanity" and the 2016 Outstanding Community Service Award by the Urban League of Greater Hartford.

Dr. Hoag created and directed the groundbreaking Developing Tomorrow's Professionals (DTP) program for black and Hispanic young men.

Stephen Hoag is the author of *A Son's Handbook: Bringing Up Mom with Alzheimer's/Dementia*, a stirring personal account of his ten years caring for his mother with this dreaded disease.

In 2018, Dr. Hoag's romantic novel, *Whisper of a Kiss*, was released with the inspirational moving book *Vows* in 2020, winning acclaim for its emotional acumen and encouraging approach to understanding one person's impact on another. His 2021 book, *Before the Picture Fades*, is a historical account of the hundred-plus-year life of Wallingford, Connecticut's Lyman Hall High School, detailing the most dramatic athletic moment in Connecticut schoolboy history.

CPSIA information can be obtained
at www.ICGtesting.com
Printed in the USA
LVHW030330180423
744563LV00002B/410